Birthright

Birthright

JEANETTE BAKER

TOP READS PUBLISHING, LLC
Vista, California USA

First Edition

ISBN: 978-1970107296 (paperback)
ISBN: 978-1970107302 (ebook)

Library of Congress Control Number: 2022909721

Birthright is published by:
Top Reads Publishing, LLC
1035 E. Vista Way, Suite 205
Vista, CA 92084 USA

For information please direct emails to:
info@topreadspublishing.com

Cover design, book layout and typography: Teri Rider & Associates
Author photo: Victoria Baker Riley

Printed in the United States of America

DEDICATION

This book is dedicated to my late father, a very special man and gifted storyteller who taught his children to appreciate the power of the written word. Although he left this world much too early, his presence remains mighty in the eyes of those who knew him.

These are among my favorite of his expressions:

Remember to practice silence. No one learns anything by listening to himself speak.

Never borrow or sell to friends. Friendship is priceless. Money and goods are not.

Travel is an education in itself. Travel often. You will come home grateful and much wiser than when you left.

Always save a dollar or two for the cup of a man in need.

Be kind to your pets. Children will learn from you.

Rest in peace, Dad.

PROLOGUE

San Juan Capistrano, California
〜Claire

It is pride and self-doubt that shaped her, signaling her heart to pound, her hands to sweat, and the inevitable stain of red heat spreading from the bone-pale skin of her chest to her forehead. Pride was her Achilles' heel, bred into her gene pool like fine wavy hair, small elfin ears, and a palate so refined she can identify a hint of spice, a pinch of cardamom, a thread of saffron, a sprinkle of coriander in the most complicated of culinary dishes.

It is that same pride, kneaded and reformatted now that she's left childhood far behind, that prevented her from disclosing to her bewildered parents when she wasn't invited to a birthday party, selected for a spot on the tennis team, or a role in a school play. Claire preferred to withhold all information, to report back after the fact, or not at all, depending on the outcome. She knew, early on, that she could upend them with the smallest hint of her inadequacy, of not belonging, of shame, fearing that it was something they had done, something defective that could never quite measure up no matter how great their efforts. They could not have their own children after all.

Because she loved and appreciated her parents, two kindly people who adopted her as an infant, and because she came to realize that suppressing details of her life evolved into self-doubt, theirs more than hers, she worked on eliminating the instinct to withdraw, the result being that for years now she was able to share a reasonable amount of herself with the three most important living members of her family: her father, her brother, and her husband, Martin. There was her niece, Lizzie, recently turned twenty—and, therefore, officially an adult—however, Liz was still in that stage of egocentricity, requiring nothing from Claire, or anyone for that matter, other than to provide a sounding board for her own issues. Lizzie didn't really count, not yet. So far it had worked well, her efforts and her family's lowering their expectations, a little give and take on both ends.

That was before the email that changed everything, the response he'd sent and she answered, and the letters that followed, two letters that were ignored rather than sent back. Returned letters would have been far more acceptable because it opened the possibility that the address was wrong or the person deceased instead of too disinterested to bother replying.

She mailed the second letter six months ago, long enough to warrant a reply, or at least an explanation. It was time to move forward or back off completely and never know. But this time, it would be harder, the moving forward part. This time the innocent might not recover. Thank God her mother was dead.

ONE

Tralee, Co. Kerry, Ireland
~*Norah*

Look at the time, half-eight, and not a child in the house washed. The expression was my late mother's, voiced nearly every day in the house where I grew up, ten children tucked into two bedrooms with one bath upstairs.

We were never close, my mother and me, not for any particular reason I can remember; we just didn't get on. It was Fiona and Kathleen she preferred, and Jimmy, always Jimmy, her middle child, the *ciotogach*, the red-headed lefty of our family who wasn't supposed to amount to much and ended up in America with more in the bank than all of us put together.

The funny thing is Jimmy loved Tralee, still does, more than Keith or Liam or Michael, certainly more than I ever did. I was desperate to immigrate and wouldn't have come back, not after Boston, but some things can't be planned and shouldn't be remembered.

Never mind all that, my mother would say. *Memories never emptied the sink or hung out the washing. All they're good for is regret.* She was right. I know now that she was a font of wisdom I didn't appreciate. It was my dad I preferred, the jokester, the man's man, always ready with a wink, a story, and a pint. Even when he told me bees could be captured in a can without a lid because they never looked up, and I tried it and nearly died from the experience, I blamed myself and never doubted him. Interesting how perspectives change as the years add up.

Speaking of the washing, it's a good day for it—breezy without a hint of rain. I'm moving slowly today, feeling unsettled, looking for an excuse to avoid housework. Fergus Murphy, the postman, on his way to the door, is as fine a reason as any to sit down for a pot of tea and a scone.

"Good morning, Mrs. Malone," he calls out. "How is the day treating you so far?"

"It's a bit early to weigh in on the day, Mr. Murphy. Have you time for a cup of tea? It's just made, and the scones are fresh."

He scratches his head, checks to see that his few remaining wisps of hair are positioned over the shiny dome of his head, and winks. "Wasn't I just thinking how I'd like one of Mrs. Malone's scones?"

"Come in, then." I hold the door for him. "Mind the step and sit down." I pour two cups of tea and set out the butter, a fresh knife, spoons, and the milk jug. "I hear that Bridget Walsh's son came home for good this time. Did his marriage go bad?"

"Isn't it an awful shame?" he replies. "They're different about marriage in America, replacing husbands and wives the same as they do their automobiles."

As far as I'm concerned, people in Ireland aren't any different when it comes to replacing a spouse, only we don't bother to make it legal. We just up and move in with someone else. But I won't get any information by speaking my mind. "It is a shame," I agree. "Poor Billy Walsh. She's a lovely girl, though, isn't she?" I refill his cup. He finishes one scone and eyes mine. "Would you like another scone, Mr. Murphy?"

"If you don't mind, Mrs. Malone. This is a particularly delicious batch."

"As I was saying, Mr. Murphy, Sheila Walsh is a lovely girl. I can't imagine why Billy would leave her."

"I heard it isn't Billy who did the leaving."

"Did you?"

"Aye. Word has it she's tired of Billy's drinking, that and no work for more than two years. Those American girls have expectations."

"As we all should, Mr. Murphy."

He drains the last of his tea. Only a few crumbs

remain of the scone. "A pint now and then can be tolerated if a man brings home his earnings."

I nod. "True enough. Given the circumstances, I can't be too sorry for Billy Walsh."

"We mustn't be too hard on him, Mrs. Malone. A second chance may be just what he needs."

A second chance with a mother who would wash his clothes, cook his meals and pick up after him. What a pity we aren't all so lucky. Another sentiment I'll keep to myself. If I collect a shilling every time I bite my tongue to keep the words in, I'll be living in an estate in Ballyard. Instead, I smile. The postman has taken enough of my time.

"Have a wonderful day, Mr. Murphy. Watch out for the dog living second next door. His bark is worse than his bite, but you never know."

"I'll do that, Mrs. Malone." He reaches into his bag and draws out an envelope. "I have a letter for you, all the way from America."

"I'll take it off your hands, thanks very much." I stuff it into the pocket of my apron, hoping he hasn't noticed the trembling of my hands.

He tips his hat. "My pleasure, Mrs. Malone. Tell himself I said hello. I hope he's helping you here at home now that he's taken redundancy."

"He is, and I will. Mind the step." It takes enormous effort to smile and wave and watch him pass the house. I shut the door tightly and pull out the envelope. I don't recognize the writing. Would I know it if I saw it? Would someone write *after nearly fifty years?* The return address says California. Funny, I can't see him in California. He'll always be Boston to me, that city of uncompromising divisions, Southie and the North End, Beacon Hill and Roxbury, segregated neighborhoods amid the bluest blood in America, which, if you think about it, isn't really very blue at all. Yes, Boston is a fitting place for lace-curtain Irish with immigrating sons, like the O'Sullivan family.

I tear the side open and pull out the single sheet of paper. I don't bother with the body of the letter, my eyes finding and focusing on the closing—the signature. Relief and the smallest hint of disappointment weaken my knees, and I sit down quickly. Of course, it isn't him. What do I expect after all this time?

I turn my attention to the letter. Who on earth is Claire Williams, and what does she want? The only people I know in America aren't speaking to me.

Minutes later, I manage to find my way to the toilet and lock the door. Fumbling with the lid, I let it fall into place and sit down heavily. I know I'm breathing. I must be breathing, or else I'd be dead. *Dear, almighty God! I'm sixty-nine years old. How could this happen? Surely after five decades, I ought to be safe. Damn those nuns.*

Several hours later, I wait for the second half of another double ring. Brigid must be out. Where does a woman go at half seven in the evening when there are children in the house? I am about to ring off when she picks up the phone. "Brigid here."

"Hello, love. It's me. Where have you been? I've been calling all evening."

"I was picking up the takeout. Is something wrong?"

"No, nothing," I swallow, catching my breath. "How are you? Any news?"

"Not really. How do you mean, news?"

"You know, the job or the children?"

There is a brief silence on the other end. Then, "We spoke yesterday, Mom."

"Did we?" I laugh, self-consciously. "I didn't realize." I wait for her to speak. "Well, if you're busy."

"We're about to eat. Shall I ring you back?"

"No, don't bother. I'll check in later this week." Carefully, I set down the phone. Nearly three hours of daylight left. Maybe I should drive to Derrymore and walk on the strand. From the sitting room, I can hear the familiar sound of Mariam O'Callaghan on RTE. After nearly fifty years of marriage, Eamon is as predictable as the Eucharist on Sunday. Why am I so fidgety? Silly question. It's the letter from that woman, Claire Williams. How did she know where to find me? No one who knows me would say anything, no one but Jimmy, and he knows the least of all. Jimmy was always one to be taking up the cause, never mind if it was someone else's business.

I bite my lip, instantly ashamed. It isn't Jimmy's fault. Even though we were close once, I'd never confided in my younger brother, never told anyone, not really. Somehow, they just found out. It's the way we do things in my family. *Say nothing, and maybe it will all go away* is our motto. Only my two older brothers know about those disastrous years in Boston when I was half out of my mind with love and shame and no one to help me. I don't blame them. It's clear why they did what they did. I see the wisdom in it and would do the same if it happened to anyone else. Perhaps I'll call Jimmy just to chat. If only it wasn't so dear to call America. We haven't spoken in years. The reason escapes me now. Some families are like that.

Eamon shouts from his chair in the sitting room. "Any chance of a cup of tea, Norah?"

I sigh, fill the electric kettle, rinse the teapot with hot water and begin assembling the tray. Tea means a full pot accompanied by milk and sugar and pastry. Eamon likes his sweets. Nothing changes. Most of the time, I prefer it that way: no challenges, no surprises, no embarrassing moments, just a long-buried secret that, if revealed, would change the course of my life. One minute I'll be Norah Malone, wife, mother, and grandmother from a well-respected family in Tralee, and the next, *everything I claim to be will be exposed for the lie it is.*

I carry the tray into the sitting room and set it on the table in front of my husband.

He sees the single cup. "Aren't you having any?"

"Not now. I thought I'd go for a walk on the strand."

"It's a bit late for that, isn't it?"

"Maybe," I admit. "Maybe not."

I fill his cup, and he looks at me. "Are you feeling poorly, Norah?"

"Why do you ask?"

"You're not sounding like yourself."

I come up with a partial truth. "I miss Brigid."

"Go see her. It isn't expensive if you're worried about the money."

Eamon is a good man, not my first choice, but a good man, better than most, certainly better than the one I nearly threw it all away for. "I'll think about it."

He teases me. "Maybe you're thinking while the cat's away, the mouse will play."

I chuckle to show him I understand he doesn't mean it. "Not in a million years, Eamon. I don't have to worry about that with you."

"I'm not so much to look at anymore, but maybe someone would have me." He is no longer looking at me.

Quick tears spring to my eyes. I curve my hand around his cheek. "There's more than a few would have you, Eamon Malone. You're a fine-looking man, and you're a true one. I consider myself a very fortunate woman to have a man like yourself."

The blood rises in his face. "We're serious for a Tuesday," he says. "Go along now and take your walk on the strand."

TWO

San Juan Capistrano, California
〜*Claire*

Tomorrow there will be fog. Today, a suffocating heat hesitates briefly over the small mission town of San Juan Capistrano before moving east, settling into the less affluent communities, the gullies, canyons, and arroyos stitched into the sides of the San Bernardino mountains. Bordering Father Junipero Serra's two-hundred-year-old mission, the heartbeat of *El Camino Real*, Avenue of the Kings, white-washed haciendas topped with tile roofs and cooled by thick adobe walls open to patios of color and movement, ribbons of light and deep velvety shade. The Basilica bells ring on the hour. Dark-skinned children dressed in school uniforms—girls with their hair tightly braided, and boys, school bags slung over one shoulder—surge on to streets powdered with the dust of purple jacaranda blossoms.

Claire opens her state-of-the-art commercial refrigerator, fills a tall glass with iced tea, pinches a sprig of mint from the herb garden blooming in her bay window, and, after dropping it into her drink, picks up her notebook, opens the French doors, and steps outside, relishing the cool, terra cotta tiles under her bare feet. She inhales. A star jasmine perfumes dry air. Purple clematis creeps across an adobe wall enclosing the still aqua of a kidney-shaped pool. Mature bougainvillea wind around patio posts forming a shaded arbor of blood-red flame. Mexican sage blooms in clay pots. Flowering hydrangeas, their petals a deep royal blue, spill over flowerbeds. Deep green pear moss grows among the stones, and hummingbirds, rose-throated and territorial, dart among feeders while finches dive for wild seed woven into netted baskets. The ambiance is one of careless and comfortable elegance.

Claire slides into a low-slung patio chair and flips open her computer. Sipping her tea, she waits for it to boot. This is her ritual, the end of her day, a favorite moment, right up there with Kona coffee, the morning paper, and a house all to herself. The screen sharpens, and her familiar inbox opens. Casually, she scrolls through her mail, deleting advertisements, saving personal messages. Quickly, confidently, her fingers move across the keys, discarding and saving.

Suddenly they stop, freezing in suspension. She stares in disbelief at the green leaves of the Ancestry logo and the bold letters that follow. After almost two years, after telling herself it was time to give up, there is finally a response.

Still, she waits. Her hands drop into her lap. Holding on to the moment when everything is still possible, she stands and walks across the patio to where lush grass meets blooming flowers. Spotting a flaw in the perfection of her landscape, she breaks off a brown stem, then a yellow leaf, crushing them in her palm and stuffing them into the pocket of her linen capris. Her fingers touch the solid shape of her cell phone. She should call Martin … and tell him what? That for two years she's spent every free moment checking Catholic adoption sites, and, because of Massachusetts' new transparency laws, today there is a reply?

What can he say to such a long and complicated withholding? She smiles briefly, tightly. Because he is Martin, his words will be careful, soothing, as if she is the one to be protected. But he will be hurt, angry even, and he will be justified. Married people—happily married people—do not keep core truths from each other. He will ask why she changed her mind after all was said and done, after they'd agreed, together, that she would stop pursuing answers where there were none. She has no reason for her silence other than her instinct to wait until there is something to tell. And now there is, or possibly not. She looks at the steady red light on the keyboard of her computer.

Carefully, she moves to the edge of the patio chair, rests her fingers on the keyboard, opens the letter on the Ancestry site, and begins to read.

~

Two hours later, she hears the garage door open and then close. Martin is home. Because he probably hiked through mud, although mud is in short supply in the heat of a California summer, he will slip off his shoes, leaving them outside. She waits for his voice, the words always the same.

"Claire," he calls out, "I'm home."

She is chopping kale and Brussels sprouts for a salad. "In the kitchen," she replies. Leaving her task momentarily, she pours a glass of icy J. Schram into a champagne flute, hands it to him and leans in for his kiss. "You're late."

"Not too bad. It's still light." He sips his drink and sighs. "What more can a man ask for but a beautiful wife and Schramsberg?"

She smiles. "I can think of a few other things, but you have those as well. There's time to shower. The shrimp is marinating, and I still have to blanch the green beans."

"When are the Masons due?"

Claire resumes her chopping. "Actually, they canceled. It's just us tonight."

"Even better. Give me ten minutes."

Claire watches him leave the room. Ten minutes. She has ten minutes to prepare herself, to explain her need to keep him out of a loop that has been nearly an obsession. She draws a deep breath and does what she always does when attempting to bring structure to a problem. She begins an imaginary conversation, taking both sides, hers and Martin's. She knows him well, his desires, his motivations. Martin is blessedly predictable, his most endearing trait.

His hypothetical questions come easily, her responses less so. Martin is wide open, transparent, his moods clear and easily accessible. She loves him for that, and for loving her despite not understanding or agreeing with the opaque, swampy depths of her thoughts. Why, then, is she nervous? Guilt cramps her stomach. Her fingers are clumsy. Enough with the chopping. There is plenty for both of them.

Working quickly, she pours the dressing—a Dijon and lemon juice recipe she picked up at the Cordon Bleu, adds toasted pine nuts and Pecorino cheese, tosses gently, and divides the salad between two plates. She adds green beans from her garden and turns to flip the prawns sizzling in their copper skillet.

Sooner than expected, Martin returns to the kitchen smelling like soap, comb tracks evident in his thick, honey-colored hair. He filches a shrimp from the pan. "Any particular reason the Masons canceled?"

"Something came up. I think Jeremy, or maybe, Levi, had a dreadful report card. They're dealing with it."

Martin laughs. "Poor kid."

Claire is about to say, "Be grateful we don't have those problems," but stops herself. It isn't Martin who had decided against children. Sliding the shrimp on to the plates forming a perfect fan, she sets them on the table. "Do you want wine, or is the champagne enough?"

"Just water for me, thanks." He pulls out her chair before seating himself. "Everything go all right at the restaurant?"

Claire spreads her napkin on her lap. "You, first. Did the bid go well?"

"We went over the plans." He squeezes lemon over the shrimp. "Used brick and exotic plants make the yard more expensive than they want, but I think they'll go for it."

"Are they still set on the rock pool?"

He laughs. "Actually, they're reserving judgment on a pool altogether."

"That should lower their costs."

"It's impractical. They're not even home in the summer months." Tentatively, he tastes the salad, chewing slowly. "This is delicious, Claire, another masterpiece."

"Hardly, but I'll accept the compliment."

He reaches out and covers her hand with his. "It's your turn. Did you decide on a bid for the restaurant remodel?"

She hesitates. "I did, actually, but I'd like to discuss something else with you first." Seconds pass.

"I'm waiting." His eyes, warm, light-filled, settle on her face.

She forces the words out in a single breath. "I got an email today from someone who knows my birth mother." Blanching at his change of expression, she hurries to explain. "It's legitimate. It's from the Ancestry website."

"I see." Carefully, Martin sets down his fork. "I thought you'd given up on that."

"No."

"You told me you had."

"I changed my mind."

"How long has this been going on?"

Of course he would ask the elemental question. She looks directly at him, her cheeks burning. "Two years."

His jaw tenses. "Two years?"

"I'm not a child, Martin. I have every right to pursue this. It's important to me. Why can't you support me in this?"

"I have supported you. I will continue to support you, but I need ground rules."

She can't have heard him correctly. "Excuse me?"

He touches his napkin to his mouth, a brief respite before he answers. "I refuse to be on the other end of your disappointment, a disappointment that includes tears, weeks of silence, depression and, ultimately, medication. People search for their birth parents all the time while living normal lives. They don't react like you. You had a wonderful childhood. You have a loving family. You own a restaurant that is tremendously successful. We've arranged our lives to accommodate the consequences of your not knowing your birthright. I've made sacrifices. I'm not willing to take it all on again."

She stares at him. "You don't sound like yourself."

"I can assure you this is definitely me."

"What if I promise it won't be like that?"

He stands, refills his water glass with champagne and comes back to the table. "Can you do that?"

"I've done it for two years."

"Let's talk about that."

He is sounding like Martin again. She smiles. "I'd be happy to."

"After your initial request, how many replies have you had?"

"Just the one."

He shakes his head. "Claire, don't you see, this is just the beginning?"

"Of course, it is. I don't understand your objection."

"What happens if you find out where your mother is and you contact her? What then? What if she doesn't want to be found? What if she doesn't answer you? How will you feel then?"

She answers honestly. "I don't know. But this man who contacted me has answers. At least I have him. Maybe, just maybe, I'll finally know my medical history and the longevity of my parents. That's important to me."

Martin sighs. "What's important to you, Claire, is why you were given up. You won't know that. You won't know your story unless the person who gave you up tells you why she didn't keep you. That's what I'm afraid of. This is an obsession that will rule your life."

"I won't let that happen."

"You have to promise me, Claire, that you won't stalk this woman if she wants nothing to do with you. She may have a family who knows nothing about her past. You can't destroy her life."

"You mean I can't treat her the way she's treated me?"

"Yes. That's exactly what I mean!"

She pushes her plate away. "There's no need to shout, Martin. I didn't mean it that way."

He stands. "I have some work to do. I'll be in my office. Don't wait up."

Claire laces the fingers of both hands, keeping them in her lap. Her instinct is to move—to collect the plates, clear the table, clean the kitchen, start the dishwasher. But she doesn't move. Her therapist tells her to move less and think more, to concentrate on events that just happened, to reflect and make sense of them, to wait, and then wait some more.

Martin is not an angry man. Martin loves her desperately. She knows this. She knows that fear is at the root of Martin's outburst. He is afraid of losing her, the person he loves, to that other woman he doesn't understand. Claire's mouth softens. She will show him he has nothing to fear. Tomorrow, she will show him.

THREE

San Juan Capistrano, California

⌇*Claire*

"God, Aunt Claire, this smells delicious!"

Claire nods, her complete concentration on the task in front of her. "Be careful, Lizzie," she warns, looking up. "Don't forget to flip the bacon. You have to watch carefully, or it'll burn."

Liz has heard the words a thousand times. Mechanically, she turns the thick slices of bacon and moves them to the side of the grill. "What are you doing now?"

"Adding blood-orange citrus oil and a pinch of Ethiopian curry salt."

"Do you think you'll have any soup left over?"

"Probably not. Soup is usually gone well before closing time."

"Not even for a taste?"

Claire laughs. Lizzie's twenty years completely disappear when she wants something. "I think I can arrange a taste." She dips a clean spoon into the soup and holds it to her niece's lips. "Try this and tell me what's in it."

Liz takes the spoon, blows gently and tastes. She tilts her head to one side, setting the copper ponytail in motion, and considers. "Pumpkin, I think, for the base, cinnamon, sugar, nutmeg, cream and, probably," she hesitates, "cardamom."

"Perfect!" Claire claps her hands. "You have an exceptional palate. I'm impressed."

"Thanks." Liz changes the subject. "What do you think Dad would say if I told him I was changing my major?"

"To what?" Claire returns to the soup. "Watch the bacon."

Liz turns back to the grill and carefully lifts the rasher to a paper towel. "Do we save the fat?"

"Not this time. But you can crumble the bacon." Claire adds creamy goat cheese to a small soufflé cup and drizzles a tablespoon of maple syrup over her creation.

Liz resumes the conversation. "I want to go to chef's school, to the Culinary Institute in particular."

Claire frowns. "That's not changing your major; that's dropping out of college." Denis O'Brian isn't an unreasonable parent, but after spending nearly forty thousand dollars a year on tuition alone, he's entitled to some return on his investment.

Liz slides the chopped bacon into a small bowl and hands it to Claire. "It's not as expensive as Marymount."

"Most of the students at culinary schools have undergraduate degrees."

"I don't need a degree to cook."

"What makes you think that?" Claire turns off the flame under the soup. "A chef is more than a cook, Lizzie. You know that. You need math and chemistry, accounting, marketing and a grasp of economics. Everyone who attends an accredited culinary school wants a restaurant, a hotel or their own business. You do need a degree for that. If you don't have the tools, success is nearly impossible." She reaches across the island and pushes a dangling wisp of hair behind her niece's ear. "Why not wait until graduation and see how you feel?"

"So, I'm supposed to waste two years of my life before I can begin learning what I want. Is that what you're saying?"

Claire sighs. "You're going to live a very long time, Liz, and you know very well that's not what I mean at all. You certainly have a handle on drama. Maybe you should major in theater."

"Who should major in theater?" Denis O'Brian stands in the doorway, tie stuffed into his pocket, jacket thrown over one shoulder. "Something smells delicious."

Liz swallows audibly. "Hi, Dad. What are you doing here?"

"Mom said Claire was driving you home. I thought I'd give your aunt a break and pick you up myself. Your car won't be ready until tomorrow. The alignment is off." He grins. "Are you driving over sidewalks?"

"Of course not."

Claire moves toward the refrigerator. "Whatever the reason, it's nice to see you. How about something cold to drink?"

"I don't want to interrupt anything if you're busy."

"Not at all." Claire pulls out a pitcher of pomegranate iced tea and pours him a glass. "We're finished. Liz is developing quite a palate."

Denis smiles. "That's my girl."

Liz sees her advantage. "The thing is, Dad, I'm thinking of chef's school."

"Great idea. Maybe you'll open a chain of restaurants and support your parents."

"What would you think of my going now?"

His smile fades. "Where would you find the time? You're in college."

"I'd like to replace college with chef's school."

He shakes his head. "Not a good idea. You have plenty of time to do both if that's what you really want. A little maturity doesn't hurt in an interview."

Lizzie's lip tightens. "Do you have any objections to me applying to the Culinary Institute in Napa?"

"I don't see the point."

"I'd like to see if I could qualify."

Denis's eyes meet Claire's. Lifting his glass, he swallows the tea, every gulp in syncopation with the leap of his Adam's apple. When the glass is drained, he appeals to his sister. "What do you think about this, Claire?"

Claire sighs. "I think Liz has natural talent, but that won't go away. I'd like to see her finish college first."

Denis relaxes and turns his attention back to his daughter. "I think that's sound advice."

"I'd like to apply anyway," Liz persists. "If they don't think I have what it takes, I should be thinking about something else. Wouldn't it be better to know that now and change my plans rather than set my sights on something that isn't likely to happen?"

Denis frowns, an expression he assumes when he wants to appear as if he's thinking deeply. Claire knows better. He has no intention of agreeing with his daughter.

"Where will you get the money?" he asks.

Lizzie's eyes widen. "What money?"

"I assume there will be an application fee. Why don't you check on that, and we can discuss it when you know."

"It can't be much. I'll take it out of my allowance."

Denis nods. "Like I said, we'll talk about it when you have all the facts."

He turns his attention to his sister. "How's the search going?"

"Nothing much, yet." Her eyes, seawater blue, meet Denis's brown ones. "Come into the study with me. I want to show you something."

"What's up?" he asks when she closes the doors of the sun-washed room. "Why all the secrecy?"

"I don't support this notion of Lizzie's, Denis, but I don't think you should lie to her. You have no intention of paying for culinary school."

"Not now, but I'm buying time, and I want to avoid an unnecessary argument. Lizzie's plans change by the hour. You know that, Claire. Is that why you wanted to talk to me?"

"No." She opens the top drawer of her desk, pulls out a folded piece of paper and hands it to him. "Read that and tell me what you think."

He unfolds the letter, reads it once and then again. Whistling softly, he hands it back to her. "Is this legitimate?"

"Yes. I think so. He's from Tralee, and he says he knows a Norah O'Connor who fits my description."

"What are you going to do?"

"I haven't decided. What would you do?"

"That has nothing to do with it."

"Of course it does. I'm asking your opinion. You're my brother."

He waits a full minute, studying her face. "No," he says gently. "At least not the way you would like. We're very different. We share a family and an upbringing but not a gene pool. No one is more cognizant of that than you are, Claire. I'm not the one searching for the mother who gave me up for adoption. I have no need to understand her motives. I'm comfortable in my own skin."

"And I'm not?"

He shakes his head. "No, you're not, and I'll prove it to you. If someone called me tomorrow and said she was my birth mother and could we meet, I'd do it if it was convenient, just out of curiosity. I'd pay for her coffee, listen to her story, walk her to her car and tell her I'd be in touch. But I probably wouldn't. People come in and out of our lives all the time. Mothers are different. We don't just pick them up on a street corner over a cup of coffee. We had a great mother, and she died two years ago. That's enough for me. I'm sorry if that seems cold, but there it is."

"So, you think I should throw this away and get on with my life?"

"No. I think you should satisfy your curiosity. Clearly, it's what you want."

Her laugh is hollow. "Martin thinks I'm insane. He's not at all happy about this."

"It isn't Martin's decision to make." He softens and slides an arm around her shoulders. "Don't worry. He'll come around."

She nods.

"Don't expect too much, Claire."

"What do you mean?"

He hesitates. "Don't have expectations. I don't want you to be disappointed. Rarely does this kind of situation have a Hollywood ending."

"I'm looking for answers, Denis, that's all. I don't want to be embraced by strangers."

"Don't you?"

She shakes her head. "I don't think so."

He smiles. "Come on. Let's get back to the kitchen. Lizzie will accuse us of arranging her future without her."

FOUR

San Juan Capistrano, California
~Claire

Claire bypasses the restaurant kitchen, ignoring the recent addition of gleaming copper pots hanging from the ceiling and the newly hung pale yellow and cornflower blue wallpaper. The café has done well this year. She opens the refrigerated display case and sets the tray of passion fruit tarts on the top shelf. Then she hesitates. What else is she supposed to do? She waits, hoping it will come to her. This happens too much lately. Her mind is not on food.

Margot, her assistant, pushes her gently out of the way and pulls out a cake. "It's the Bouche Noelle for Mrs. Grayson's daughter." She speaks softly. "It's her favorite birthday cake which is why we made it out of season."

Claire glances at the chocolate and cream roll and sighs. "Sorry, Margot. I'm not myself lately."

"Anything I can do?"

She shakes her head. "Take the cake to Mrs. Grayson and wish her daughter a happy birthday. I'll be in my office looking over the invoices. Interrupt if you need me."

The office is small. Claire spends little time here. Most of her work is done at home in the spacious, light-filled room facing the patio. But today, Martin is home, and although he hasn't mentioned it again, she would rather not stir up the subject of her birth mother and the potential trip to Ireland. She pulls her chair close so that her back is straight and tight against the chair, waiting for the computer to boot. Her fingers hover over the keyboard, her mind searching for the right words, the appropriate words, a fine line that won't encourage but also won't minimize the effort of the man she's come to know as Kevin. His curiosity is unusual for someone only remotely involved. Still, he's done a great deal of research on her behalf, and it's only natural for him to want to share it with her, but she's not sure she's ready for all of it at once. The letter to the woman she believes is her birth mother has gone unanswered, and the silence has shaken her confidence. The situation is disappointing but not entirely unexpected. Still, Claire isn't sure she wants to dig any deeper just yet, not without Martin. If only he was on board. They could travel to Ireland together, spend some time in Tralee, see the lay of the land, so to speak.

Twenty minutes later, she clicks on the submit tab and stands, rubbing the small of her back. She wants to go home. It's nearly closing time, and everything is under control here at the café. It's Friday, and Martin will be wondering where she is. Now is as good a day as any to put out feelers regarding a trip to Ireland.

Claire unlocks the door, picks up the mail piling on the floor and walks into the kitchen. "Hello. Anybody home?" The house is quiet, empty, cool but welcoming. Where is Martin?

She pours herself a glass of Perrier, rubs a lime quarter around the edge, squeezes a few drops of juice into the glass, steps out onto the patio and sinks into a chair. Resting her head against the high back, she closes her eyes and imagines her birth mother. As always, she creates her in the image of herself: slim, small-boned with dark wavy hair and blue-green eyes, a woman who makes mistakes but forges ahead, a happy woman, content with her life except for the hole left by the absence of her first child, a daughter she was forced to give up.

"Claire," Martin's voice calls out to her. "Where are you?"

Jerked from her reverie, she blinks. "In the back."

He steps through the doors, leaving them open

and sits down beside her. "I'm beat. I hope you didn't have plans tonight."

"I thought I'd make something simple, pasta and salad."

Nodding, he takes a sip of her drink and sighs. "Perfect."

She glances at his worn blue jeans and chambray shirt. "It looks like you were in the field today. What happened?"

"Nothing that hasn't happened nearly every week since I took on the Marshalls. She has one idea, her husband has another. They can't come up with a time to meet with me, at least not together; therefore, nothing is ever negotiated, and we continue to battle over the same issues. I don't need this. Maybe, we should take a vacation and give them time to find someone else."

Claire stares at him. "They're your friends, Martin. Do you really mean that?"

"Why not? We could both use a break. What do you think?"

She wets her lips. "Actually, I was thinking the same thing." She speaks quickly, before she loses her nerve. "I'd like to go to Ireland, to Tralee, and meet the man I've been communicating with, maybe even the woman he believes is my mother."

Martin's mouth tightens. "She hasn't answered your letters, Claire. She doesn't want to hear from you."

"You can't know that."

"The woman won't respond to you. Explain to me how you see the situation."

Claire speaks slowly, fighting off the hurt that his words call up. "If she has nothing to hide, she would have answered me. She would have told me she isn't related to me, and that would have been it. Clearly, she is my birth mother."

"But she has no intention of encouraging you."

"I just want to see her, Martin. I don't even need to tell her who I am. All I want is to know how she lives and what she looks like."

He shakes his head. "That isn't true, sweetheart. You want her to want you, to apologize for giving you up and to welcome you into her family."

Claire blinks back tears, pulls her sunglasses from her pocket and puts them on. "So, where did you have in mind?"

"Excuse me?"

"You said you wanted a vacation," she reminds him. "Where do you want to go?"

"Somewhere warm and lazy, Hawaii, maybe, or Fiji."

Her laughter carries an edge. "We live in California, Martin. It's warm *here*."

His eyes fill with pity and something else she doesn't recognize. "Maybe, we should table the vacation idea until we have some time to think about it."

She nods and looks away, staring at the hot, bright colors of the bougainvillea climbing the stucco wall.

Without speaking, Martin stands, rests his hand briefly on her shoulder, then disappears into the house.

FIVE

San Juan Capistrano, California
⁓ *Claire*

"Any chance of a cup of coffee and one of those butter-filled things I'm not supposed to eat?"

Claire knows that voice and to whom it belongs. She smiles, shuts down the computer in her office and looks at her father. "I can even offer you some company while you enjoy them."

Michael O'Brian kisses his daughter's cheek. "All the better."

"So, Dad," she begins when they are seated in a quiet window booth in the corner of her cafe, "what brings you here today?"

"I called to see if you wanted to meet me for lunch and, somehow, mixed up your number with Martin's."

She waits patiently while he slathers butter over the delicate pastry. Michael O'Brian, always thorough and to the point, can't be nudged from whatever task is at hand.

Finally, he looks up. "What's this about contacting your birth mother?"

Claire releases her breath. "Did Martin tell you he's against it?"

"Not in so many words."

She stirs cream into her coffee and pushes it away without drinking it. "Well, he is. What else did he say?"

"He's worried you won't be able to handle the rejection."

"And?"

"And nothing. That's all."

"Do you agree with him?"

"On the contrary. In your entire life, you've never admitted defeat. I don't imagine this would take you down."

Claire relaxes. "Thank you."

"However," he bites into his croissant, chews and swallows before continuing. "I'm wondering why you aren't handling this with your usual aplomb."

"What do you mean?"

"Martin sounds insecure and slightly angry. How did you allow this to happen?"

Claire sighs. She loves this man, and normally, his forthright temperament brings her relief, settling into place the pieces of what she doesn't understand. Today, she is simply irritated. "I'm not following you, Dad."

"Why all the secrecy, Claire? Why don't you simply share what you're doing with Martin, even give him a role? He feels completely left out of something you feel is of utmost importance. That isn't the way a good marriage works."

"Maybe we don't have a good marriage."

Her father's face softens. "Martin has made some difficult sacrifices to be with you, Claire. He needs an occasional stroke. You know that, and you've always complied. What's so different about this search of yours? Why the big mystery and dramatic revelation?"

She shrugs. "It wasn't exactly a plan. Everything escalated when I got the email. I didn't know whether to believe it or not. Martin has never been particularly thrilled with anything related to my search. He would have said, 'I told you so.' He doesn't understand why I'm doing it, and as far as making sacrifices, he's not the only one." Her voice breaks. "I don't think you or Martin understand."

He reaches for her hand. "It doesn't matter that we do or don't. We want the best for you and if you think finding the woman who gave birth to you will change your life, so be it. We'll support you." He frowns. "I'm mad at myself for not insisting on more specifics. It just wasn't something I even thought about. I gave your birth mother my card assuming she might want to contact you, but I didn't ask for anything in return. I'm so sorry, Claire."

"It's not your fault. I wouldn't be doing this if Mom was alive. She was so against my searching. Her eyes would water whenever I mentioned it."

"She was afraid of losing you."

"I know. I wish she had trusted me."

"You'll find a way. Remember, Claire, Martin is in for the duration. Not everyone finds that. Don't throw it away."

Claire draws back. "My God, is it that serious? You make it sound as if I'm having an affair, and he's thinking of leaving me."

Michael O'Brian laughs, refuses another cup of coffee and stands. "I know when you're stonewalling, my love. You're smart enough to get the result you say you want. However, I have my doubts that it's what you *really* want." Heading toward the door, he rests his hand briefly on her head. "Good luck with this. Let me know if I can help."

"Dad?" Claire hesitates.

He is nearly out the door. "Yes?"

"You're not keeping anything from me, are you?"

"Of course not. Why would you ask such a thing?"

She shakes her head slowly. "No, reason, really. But it isn't like you to leave so much up in the air."

"What do you mean?"

Her eyes meet his. "This is the first time you mentioned that you'd actually met my birth mother. You knew who she was, but you never told me. Why not?"

"Honestly, I never thought it was that important to you. You're a very private person, and you hold a great deal inside. I had no idea finding Norah O'Connor was your lifelong quest. If you had confided in me, I would have told you what I know."

"Even if Mom didn't want me to have that information?"

"Yes."

"I do have a question."

He waits.

"Do I look like her?"

He shakes his head. "I remember a slender woman with brown hair and fair skin. You were a chubby baby. At the time, I didn't notice a resemblance. It was a long time ago. I'm sorry."

"Never mind. It doesn't matter." She smiles at him. "See you later."

Claire stares out the window at the overcast sky for a full fifteen minutes after her father had gone. Then, as if coming to a decision, she looks at her watch, finishes her now lukewarm coffee and heads back to her office for her purse. It is time to stand up for herself.

SIX

⤳Norah

Damn this dress. It fit when I bought it. I turn to look at my backside in the small mirror over the basin. Horrified at the rolls of flesh evident above and below my bra strap, I suck in my stomach. A bit better, but not much. There's no help for it. I must give up the crisps and maybe even the chips, too.

Eamon calls from outside the door. "About ready, Norah?"

"In a tick." I pull the material snugly over my hips. Surely, I have a black pullover somewhere. The bulges aren't so bad that a pullover won't hide them.

"Do you think I've gained weight, Eamon?" I ask, standing before him, breathless from my efforts. "Be honest with me, now."

"Not at all." He shakes his head vigorously. "You've

a fine figure for a woman your age. We all put on a bit after a few years."

"In other words, your answer is yes?"

He looks astonished. "How did you come by that? I never said it."

It is too late to argue. The ten-thirty Mass is always full. As it is, we'll have to fight for a seat. My father, may he rest in peace, called it the slacker's Mass. "Never mind. Help me into this pullover. Do you think the children have any intention of joining us?"

Eamon chuckles as he guides my left arm into the sleeve. "They're a bit old to expect them to come with us, Norah. I'm sure they attend according to their own schedules."

He really is a sweet man, but completely oblivious. James and Patricia haven't seen the inside of a church since the Christmas before last, and as for Brigid, you'd think a mother would want her children to take their first communion and be confirmed, but if Brigid has reformed, she keeps it a well-guarded secret.

St. John's Church smells like wet wool—the cause, a heavy morning rain and the subsequent, unseasonal heat that followed. I am stuck between Eamon and an old woman who mutters to herself while constantly fidgeting in her handbag. Away with the faeries, she is. It's a disgrace that services for the demented have been cut yet again. Maybe James and Patricia have the right idea. After all, I've been to enough Masses in my life. Skipping a few now and then can't hurt. But then, maybe I have more to make up for.

Normally, I don't care for incense, but today anything is better than the sheep smell coming off the farmers. The priest, a guest by the look of him, is flanked by three altar boys and one girl. No problem with Catholics allowing girls to participate at the lowest levels, just as long as they're happy serving.

The opening hymn over, I settle in beside Eamon and prepare myself for the Introductory Rites. Eyeglasses would help, but the tight seating prevents me from searching my handbag. The guest priest is officially from the States, but his accent is pure Tralee.

"The grace of our Lord Jesus Christ and the love of God and the fellowship of the Holy Spirit be with you all."

Mechanically, I respond, "And also with you."

"Dear friends, this water will remind us of our baptism. Let us ask God to bless it and to keep us faithful to the Spirit he has given us." He picks up the aspergillum and steps down from the altar, sprinkling water on worshippers in the first row, then the second.

A minute passes, and then another. I have the strangest feeling I know this man. I need a better look at him. Straining my eyes, I lean toward Eamon and then toward the odd little woman on my other side. She glares at me. I pay no attention. All I can see of the visiting priest is gray hair, plenty of it, and although he doesn't look to be tall, he isn't heavy or oddly shaped. There is something about his gait and the way he turns his head.

"Eamon," I whisper. "Do we know him?"

He nods.

"Who is he?"

"Patrick O'Sullivan, from Ballyard."

I stare at him. Patrick O'Sullivan? Here? In Tralee?

I must have looked blank because he continues. "You know, the oldest of the O'Sullivan boys. His mother died recently, and the house is for sale."

"Hush!" the woman beside me whispers loudly. "This is a church, not a pub."

"Sorry," I manage, but the woman ignores me, hooks her bag over her shoulder and climbs out of the pew. Normally, her oddness would intrigue me, but not today. In a moment the priest will be upon us waving the acrid-smelling aspergillum. I feel exposed as if everyone is watching me and not the man walking among us.

He glances in my direction, his eyes passing over me as if he's never seen me before, as if I hadn't spent countless hours with him sharing every thought passing through my head. But it happens often, I suppose, the absence of recognition when you don't expect to see someone. And yet why wouldn't he? This is Tralee, my home. Where else would I go? Of course, he would expect to see me. He *should* have imagined our meeting, perhaps even prepared for it, unless too many years have passed and I'm rendered insignificant.

Deliberately, I drop my bag and dive after it, spending long seconds on the floor. I don't want his memory jogged until I'm better prepared. Damn this tight dress. I cross myself for thinking profane thoughts inside the church. He moves on. I slide back into my seat. Somehow, I manage to get through the Penitential Rite, the Kyrie and the Gloria. Finally, finally, the first two readings of the liturgy, followed by the Gospel and then, what I'd waited for, the Homily.

He speaks. "Good morning, ladies and gentlemen. I'm Monsignor Patrick O'Sullivan. Some of you may know me. I grew up here in Tralee, in Ballyard. I've spent the last fifty years in the States, but I've always wanted to come home. Now that I'm retired, my wish has come true. I've been invited by Father Meskill to say Mass here at St. John's. We haven't come up with a schedule, but if you call the parish office, Mrs. Brosnan will have all the information you need."

What is he saying? Does it matter? "Eamon," I whisper. "I'm not feeling well. I'm going home."

He frowns. "Are you sick?"

"I don't know. I think so."

"Can't you wait until he's finished, until after the Offertory?" Eamon passes the baskets. It is a duty he takes seriously. He wouldn't dream of leaving before the Offertory.

I swallow. There is no help for me. No power on Earth or elsewhere can make me stand up in that sea of people and exit the church alone, under the watchful eyes of Monsignor Patrick O'Sullivan. *Monsignor*, my arse. That one won't get closer than a light-year to the pearly gates.

SEVEN

Tralee, Co. Kerry, Ireland
⤳Norah

"Are you feeling better, Norah?" Eamon is all attention now that his role is finished, for this week at least.

I ignore his question. "Thank goodness it's just the two of us. I can't bear the thought of cooking for a mob, not today."

"Two children isn't exactly a mob."

"Maybe not, but husbands, wives and children are. Besides, it doesn't matter. They're not coming over."

Eamon thinks a minute. "Would you like to drive out to Dingle and have lunch?"

"That's a lovely idea, Eamon, but the weather's bad. It's close to raining now."

"If we let a bit of rain bother us, we wouldn't go anywhere at all."

I relent. "I've heard there's a nice restaurant on the main road, the Blue something."

"Shouldn't be hard to find. We can always find a seat in Danno's."

I bite my tongue. It is a nice gesture. If I want more of them, I mustn't criticize.

The rain holds off, and the drive is lovely, with occasional patches of sunlight coloring the hills that brilliant green that brings Ireland its summer tourists. Branching off at the Derrymore Cross, Eamon is blessedly silent while I take in the changing sky, the churning sea, a herd of unusually marked cows—Galloways, black with what looks like a white towel around their middles, and the herald of spring in Ireland, yellow daffodils around every curve of the road. It is more than lovely. It is mood-changing. Why don't we drive out on Sunday more often, I wonder?

Passing the Skellig Hotel, the town's landmark, we round the bend and find a carpark close to the road with space to spare. Eamon parks, rummages in the boot for the umbrella and helps me out. I squint, hold up my hand against the blinding sun and look first up and then down the main street. "The houses look freshly painted. Do you think they are?"

"Probably not." Eamon's hand is on my shoulder. It is something he does for guidance or connection; I don't know which. I wonder if he thinks he'll lose me if we walk like normal people. For some reason, he doesn't really like holding hands.

I look again at the oranges, the blues, the purples and yellows that color the houses and storefronts of Dingle. "I don't remember them being so clean and bright."

"It's just rained, and the sun is shining. Maybe we never hit both at the same time before."

It's always raining in Ireland, and most of the time the sun comes out after. More likely than not, we'd hit both many times before. I caught my retort before giving it voice. Why am I always so critical of Eamon? He means no harm. It's just conversation after all. When he had the gall bladder surgery last year, it nearly killed me to think of losing him. Not that gall bladder surgery kills people very often. Still, we didn't know in the beginning. It could have been something serious. I smile at him. "I'm hungry."

Eamon nods at a blue storefront. "Is that the restaurant you were thinking about, Out of the Blue?"

"It is. You found it. Aren't you the smart one?"

He glances at me with an odd expression on his face. Maybe finding a restaurant on the Dingle Road as we pass by on the footpath isn't worthy of a compliment.

The restaurant, decorated with wooden benches and blue-checked table linens, is larger on the inside than it looks. Eamon orders a pint. "Are you having more than one?" I ask.

"I haven't decided yet."

"Because if you are, I'll have to drive home, so I'll stick with a pot of tea."

He sighs. "I won't have more than two."

"One's the limit, Eamon. You're not a big man."

"All right. I'll only have one and another this evening after I drive home. It's Sunday. A man likes to have a pint or two on Sunday." He opens the menu. "What will you have for a meal?"

"Fish pie with mash and vegetables." To hell with my rolls of flesh and a dress that no longer fits. "It's the special. Brigid says the special is always the one to order."

He snorts. "What does she know? More than likely it's the leftover food that no one wanted."

Normally, I would have taken issue with his comment. Brigid has worked in the restaurant business for years. She should know something. But it isn't the subject I want to discuss with him. "When did Patrick O'Sullivan come back to Tralee?"

He thinks a minute. "A week, maybe two. I saw him on the street. He stopped to talk for a bit. As a matter of fact, he asked about you."

"Me? Why on earth would he do that?"

The waiter appears at our table. "Have you decided, or shall I describe the specials?"

Eamon orders for both of us, which is just as well because, for the life of me, I can't remember what I wanted. "She'll have the fish pie with mash and vegetables, and I'll have the seafood chowder and a green salad with a bit of brown bread."

I wait for him to resume our conversation, but apparently, he's forgotten what we were discussing. I attempt to jog his memory. "I hope he wasn't implying that we were ever friends."

Eamon swallows, shakes his head and chuckles. "Not at all. You were a bit young to be part of his clique, and too poor. We all were."

I sniff. "What did he say about me?"

"Nothing much, just asked how you were and had you ever returned to Boston. He was polite, nothing more. As I said, his crowd is mostly all dead now. Too bad. He won't find Tralee as he left it."

An understatement if there ever was one.

EIGHT

San Juan Capistrano, California
⌒Claire

Liz's lip settles on the edge of the spoon, delicately tasting the chocolate sauce. Her eyes narrow, and her left hip juts out, a pose she assumes when she's evaluating. She nods and straightens. "I like it. The orange gives it a fresh, rich quality. I was worried that the tartness would overcome the creamy flavor that people want when they order chocolate, but this doesn't do that. How will you use it?"

Claire shrugs. "I'm not sure. Maybe I'll drizzle over the fruit tart or offer it in the dessert soufflé." She sighs. "I'm really tired of the soufflé. I'd like to take it off the menu."

Liz's eyes widen. "You should rethink that. It's a favorite here in the restaurant. Just because you're sick of it doesn't mean other people are. You always tell me to remember the clientele. I'm giving you back your own advice. Most palates aren't as adventurous as yours."

Claire stares at her niece. This is Lizzie, the little girl who would scream with delight and cling to her leg to prevent Claire from leaving. Somehow, she had managed to grow up under everyone's nose. "You're absolutely right," Claire replies slowly. "The soufflé stays on the menu."

Lizzie's forehead clears. "I didn't really think you'd listen to me," she confesses. "But I know I'm right."

"Do I dismiss your ideas, Liz?"

Her reply is carefully worded, diplomatic. "Sometimes," Liz admits, "but you're experienced, and I'm learning. I don't take it personally, and I don't let it stop me." She smiles sunnily. "What's this I hear about going to Ireland to confront your birth mother?"

"Is that how your dad described it, *confronting* my birth mother?"

"You know Dad."

"I do, which is why I'm surprised. It sounds more like your interpretation than his."

Liz drops the spoon in the sink and picks up another one. She takes her time dipping it into the sauce before tasting it again and licking the dark residue from her lips. "I suppose it is," she admits. "Are you really going?"

Claire turns away, gives the counter a final swipe and drops the towel into the laundry bin. "Yes. It's something I need to do. I probably won't actually meet my mother since she clearly doesn't want to connect, but at least I'll see where she lives, walk the streets, eat the food, absorb a little culture—the one I would have been born into if she'd kept me."

"That sounds like something Uncle Martin might enjoy."

Claire regrets not having something to do with her hands. "Not this time."

Liz maintains silence for the better part of a minute. "That doesn't sound good. Is everything all right, Aunt Claire?"

Claire isn't about to discuss her marriage with her niece. "It's fine, except for the restaurant."

"What about it?"

"I'll be away for two weeks, and Margot will handle most things until I get back. But I could use another pair of hands." She turns to look at Liz. "I'll hire you if you're available."

"I'd love it." Liz's eyes shine. "Will you talk to Dad?"

Claire is no match for the hope lighting up her niece's face. "I'll try, Liz," she says gently, "but if you don't have a school break, there isn't much I can do. You know how Denis feels about your education."

"I don't have class on Fridays, and I can come in on the weekend."

"I'll give it my best, and I'll pay you."

Liz laughs. "Now that's an offer I can't refuse."

~

Bleary-eyed from her sleepless night on the plane, Claire looks out the window and catches her breath. The patchwork green she's seen on every postcard of Ireland materializes below the clouds. The Shannon, bottomless and swollen from winter rain, is pure silver beneath a sky emerging from a thick, gray mist. Pale smoke circles the cottages set down in lime-rich fields, and those tiny white dots sprinkled like lint among the green must be local sheep enjoying breakfast.

Claire fills out her landing card, shows her passport and declares nothing, making her way past baggage claim in the direction of the car rental signs. Somehow, she manages to answer questions, exchange currency, find her vehicle—a make and model she's never seen before, examine the map and head south toward Tralee, careful to follow the signs indicating that traffic comes from the right.

Choosing the coast route instead of the new toll bridge, she watches the rise and fall of the hills, the twisting road before her and the brilliant green of fields separated like puzzle pieces by natural hedges. The exhaustion she felt on the plane disappears, and she feels a buzz of anticipation for the first time since she left Martin at the airport.

It wasn't a pleasant parting. She can't remember a time when they've parted without a kiss and a plan to reconnect. Martin's coolness would normally have reduced her to tears, but resentment, now grown to dangerous proportions, did not allow for anything more than a quick wave at the curb. She wanted and had actually planned an end to their separateness, a confrontation where grievances were aired and understanding gained. But upon further reflection, she decided to do nothing, to wait, just this once, for Martin to be the supplicant instead of the one bestowing forgiveness. Perhaps that wasn't a completely accurate picture of their more difficult discussions, but it does seem as if her husband can stonewall for much longer than she can. Claire realizes it is her own insecurity that demands instant reconciliation. The pattern is one that she and Martin have grown comfortable with, except that she really hasn't. Abandonment is a condition she's carried with her since the day her mother divulged that she hadn't given birth to her.

She pulls over at a convenience store and purchases a cup of tea and a fruit scone which means a biscuit studded with raisins. The milk inside her normally black tea is a surprise. She didn't expect Ireland to be so very English, but after a tentative sip, she finds the milk takes away the bitter aftertaste usually associated with hot tea. She stares out the window, inhaling the thick, water-rich air and realizes, for the first time, that she has no plan. For a woman whose life ran on time schedules, opening and closing times, meal times, delivery times and food preparation, it leaves her with a momentary feeling of emptiness. She doesn't know a soul in Tralee, and, for the first time, she is alone in a foreign country.

According to Kevin, her contact, County Kerry is rife with O'Connors—Claire's blood family. It's just that they want nothing to do with her. For some reason, the thought stirs her sense of the ridiculous. *Welcome to Tralee, Claire, but don't look anyone up.* She forces herself to laugh out loud and immediately feels better.

The constant roundabouts that replace intersections are a challenge, but Claire manages to stay in her lane and move into the line of traffic without damaging herself or anyone else. The map doesn't indicate the new bypasses that come up, one after the other, but the villages are charming, the roads are good and the Tralee signs revealing the declining mileage are frequent enough to give her confidence. She's decided against the typical tourist Bed and Breakfast and chosen The Rose, a hotel on the edge of town. At the desk, a woman checks her in and assures her that everything is within walking distance.

Alone in her room, she decides on a nap instead of texting Martin. It is ten o'clock in the morning. Kevin has promised to meet her at 3:00 p.m. at the McDonalds she passed on the edge of town. Claire falls asleep as soon as her head finds the pillow.

NINE

Tralee, Co. Kerry, Ireland
～*Claire*

Kevin sets the two coffees down and takes a seat in the booth across from her. He is a small man by American standards, not much taller than Claire, formally dressed, dark-eyed with thin gray hair, a heavily lined face and teeth too perfect to be anything but dentures. His accent is heavy with odd vowel inflections and absolutely no regard for consonant blends, especially the *th* sound. Claire, accustomed to Irish correspondents reporting the news on television, struggles to catch the meaning of his words. So far she recognizes *nort* as being *north*, and *dem* is *them*. "Do you know Norah well?" she asks after the initial introductions are over.

He draws a deep breath. "You might say that. I'm her husband. Norah O'Connor has been my wife for forty-seven years. I also have a confession to make. My name isn't Kevin. It's Eamon, Eamon Malone."

Claire takes a minute to process his information before speaking again. "Did she tell you about my letter? Is that how you knew it was me?"

"No. Norah's a great one for keeping secrets. But when I read your request on the internet, I knew you had to be Norah's daughter. It explains a great deal, you see."

Her question isn't really answered, but she decides to ignore the lapse. "Does she know I'm here in Tralee and that you're meeting with me now?"

"Norah knows nothing at all about your visit. You should have told me you were going to write to her. I found your letter in the secretary when I was looking for stamps."

"I had no idea you were so directly involved. Will you tell her I'm here?"

He nods slowly. "I wanted to wait and see if she would tell me on her own, but now that is no longer possible."

"I don't understand. What changed your mind?"

"You did. You're a dead ringer for Brigid."

"Brigid?"

"Norah's firstborn, or so I thought. She was pregnant with Brigid when I married her."

Something doesn't make sense, but Claire's mind is still foggy from lack of sleep. "I'm sorry, but I still don't understand."

Eamon interrupts her. "Brigid isn't my child. Norah was involved with someone when she lived in America. I knew that and married her anyway. We made a life together. We have two more children, James and Patricia."

Claire's mind reels. *Norah kept Brigid. She gave me away, her firstborn, but she kept Brigid.*

The man is clearly agitated. "James and Patricia are very similar," he continues. "Brigid is different, understandably. She has a different father. What makes no sense is why you're enough like her to be her twin. Shouldn't you be different from all three of them?"

"I suppose both of us look like Norah."

He shakes his head. "Not at all. You're the spit out of Brigid's mouth, or she yours, and I've done the figuring. She's not even one year younger than you."

The implication hits her with full force. She voices her thoughts to settle them in her mind. "Are you suggesting that Brigid and I have the same father, that we're enough alike for people to notice?"

He nods. "I am. Norah will know you the minute she sets eyes on you."

"How likely is that?"

"Very likely. Tralee is a town of twenty-five thousand people. Word will spread. I must tell her what I've done."

Claire stares at him in surprise. Her own involvement recedes, and for the first time, she considers the betrayal he has only just realized. "Surely, it's Norah who owes you the explanation," she says gently.

"I suppose that's one way of looking at it."

"What other way could there be?"

His face softens. "Times have changed. Fifty years ago, young, unmarried Catholic girls did not announce their pregnancies. The shame of it would kill their families. They'd be scared for their lives that someone would drag them off to a Magdalene Laundry, never to be heard from again."

She holds up her hand. "What is a Magdalene Laundry?"

"Workhouses, Mrs. Williams, run by the Catholic Church. Unmarried women who had relations with men were sentenced by their families to work as unpaid labor. Against their will, their babies were sold to Catholic families. Sometimes the women were completely forgotten and died in those houses."

"Good lord! They can't still exist?"

"The last one was shut down in 1996. They are Ireland's disgrace. The women had no one to speak for them. Surely, you can understand why a woman would want to keep that part of her life private."

All at once, Claire likes him very much. "I think Norah is very lucky to have you, Mr. Malone."

Color rises in his face. "Not at all. I'm the lucky one."

"Will you answer a question for me?"

"If I can."

"If you knew that Norah wouldn't want to see me, why did you contact me?"

Once again, he colors and waits before he speaks as if it takes great effort to form the words. "You seemed all alone," he says at last. "I thought it would be a gift I could give you, your family name, the identity of your mother, the town she lives in. I wanted to give Norah the chance to know you turned out all right and even change her mind about meeting you. You don't seem like a vengeful type of person. What harm could it do if you visited, looked around a bit and went home? Who would know? I had no idea you and Brigid would be so alike. If you stay, it will all come out." He smiles sheepishly. "Can I convince you to go home and leave us all in peace?"

Claire shakes her head. "I'm afraid not. I've come eight thousand miles at considerable expense and more than a little inconvenience. This is more important to me than you'll ever know. I've spent a lifetime wondering where I belong and to whom. One of the reasons I decided against having children is because I don't know my family's medical history. Even if I never learn why my mother gave me up, at least I'll know the rest of it." Her eyes fill, and she looks away. "I'm sorry, but you can't know what it's been like for me."

"Maybe not, but stories like yours, and much worse, are common enough here in Ireland."

"What do you mean?"

"Not too long ago, poverty was extreme here. People had ten, twelve, fifteen children and couldn't feed them. Some just up and left the oldest to fend for himself."

"Do you mean immigration?"

"No. I mean children no older than twelve would come home from school to a cleaned-out house. Their families left them behind."

"Good God, you can't be serious!"

"I'm one of those children. So, you see, Mrs. Williams, a home in America with two parents who wanted you enough to adopt you doesn't seem like too much of a tragedy to me."

"I see your point. But it won't stop me from what I came for."

He smiles. "Fair enough."

"I will assure you I have no intention of telling anyone you contacted me."

"Do as you please with that. I will be telling Norah my part in all this and that you're here and would like to see her." He holds out his hand. "It was a pleasure meeting you. Good luck to you."

Claire takes his outstretched hand. "Thank you."

TEN

Tralee, Co. Kerry, Ireland
~*Norah*

I tighten the sash of my robe, pour a cup of tea and sit down at the table. "I'm not going to Mass today, Eamon. My stomach's off. It's probably all the cream on that pie last night. I don't do so well with heavy cream anymore."

"I'll stay home with you," he volunteers.

Eamon, volunteering to skip Mass? "There's no need. I won't be good company. You go ahead."

He pours himself a cup of tea and sits down across from me. "Actually, there's something I need to tell you."

"Can't it wait?"

He thinks a minute. "No," he decides. "It can't."

I sigh. "Go on, if you must."

He looks at me with a long steady gaze, and even though I know he couldn't possibly have found out, my stomach churns. I can't look at him.

"I needed stamps from the desk." He pulls a folded piece of paper from his back pocket and lays it on the table. "I found this."

I stare at it. How could I have been so stupid? When did Eamon ever look in the secretary?

"Do you know what it is, Norah?"

"Yes."

"Do you have anything to tell me?"

Did I have anything to tell him? What did he know? I consider denying everything, but discard the idea almost immediately. "What would you like me to say, Eamon?"

"Tell me about this child."

"There's nothing to tell. I made a mistake, two of them, actually."

"You told me Brigid was the result of one night when you had too much to drink. That doesn't happen twice. You lied to me, Norah. I want the truth now."

Outside on the street, a delivery truck screeches to a stop. Boys practicing football argue over a foul. The bells of St. John's indicate the hour, and through the sheers, I can see Mr. and Mrs. Cronin, hand in hand, heading for Mass. Had Eamon and I ever held hands? Had he wanted to? Would I have accepted his gesture? So much opportunity wasted. I decide to tell him the truth, or as much of it as he needs to know. "I didn't lie, Eamon. I just didn't tell you all of it. I was ashamed to admit what I'd done, especially as I'd done it twice."

"Is there any more, Norah? Because if there is, now is the time to have it out."

He knows. I know he does, but how? "Why are you asking me this?"

His hands are in fists on the table, and his forehead clenches. "I want more than anything to let you walk into it, to watch you come up with yet another story that I know isn't true. But what purpose would it serve? I have no intention of leaving you. We've been married a lifetime. I still love you despite everything. Tell me why Claire Williams is the image of Brigid and why the two of them look nothing like you."

"What are you talking about?"

"Claire Williams is in Tralee. I met with her yesterday. She won't be leaving until she has answers, and Norah, this time she holds all the cards."

I can't stop my hands from shaking. "What are you telling me?" I whisper.

"She told me she's written twice, and you never answered. That was a mistake, Norah. You could have met her in London or Dublin. Now she's here, enough like her sister to be a twin, and everything you tried to hide won't be hidden any longer."

"You were the one I wanted it hidden from."

He shakes his head, a man no longer so easily fooled as he once was. "I doubt that. Why are they so alike, Norah, two girls not even a year apart? Who was their father?"

"What do you mean, *their* father?"

He is angry, angrier than I've ever seen him. "Don't lie this time, Norah, not now. You know what I mean. The same man fathered both of them. Who is he?"

I stand, shaken and sick as I am. "What is your part in this, Eamon Malone? Does a woman just show up and know to contact you? I'm thinking it's me who should be asking you to tell the truth."

He sighs. "I was on the internet for information on my own family. I saw Claire's request. She called herself Aoife O'Connor. She named you as her mother. She had everything right. I answered her."

I can barely speak. "You keep secrets of your own, Eamon."

He slams his fist on the table. "Don't turn this around. Why won't you tell me? What are you afraid of? Have I ever done anything to give you reason to fear me?"

"It isn't that," I whisper. "I'm not afraid of you, Eamon."

"You're afraid of something." He stops, a puzzled look on his face as if the words have meaning for the first time. "It's someone else, isn't it? You're protecting someone else."

I hide my face in my hands. "Go away, Eamon. I can't do this anymore."

He stands over me, a kind man whose reserves are pushed to the limit. "I can't make you tell me, but I will find out. You weren't alone in Boston all those years ago. Your brothers were there and a great many friends from Tralee. Someone will tell me. I only hope he's worth the trouble."

I watch him leave the kitchen and walk out the door. There are some things that can't be explained. But it isn't loyalty that keeps my mouth shut. I know that for sure. What I don't know is why, after nearly five decades, I'm still struck dumb with the shame of what happened during those first years in Boston.

ELEVEN

Boston, Massachusetts, 1962

∾Norah

Immigration was never easy, not even for those who fly to their destinations in temperature-controlled 707 jet planes complete with full-course meals, tea carts and hot towels. The O'Connor children were not encouraged to immigrate despite ten children between the ages of two and twenty-two practically living on top of each other.

Donal, the family patriarch, provided a decent, if not luxurious, living, enough to adequately feed and clothe his children as long as the oldest members understood they must contribute when the time came for them to leave school. Higher education wasn't mentioned, although a trade for those who had aptitude was encouraged. No one but Jimmy aspired in that direction. The job-for-life, in Donal's world, meant everything. The meat plant where he, a Catholic, held a managerial position was the logical choice for his offspring, but there were others offering employment opportunities for the masses who weren't intended for civil service positions; the CWS, Denny's Bacon Plant, McCowen's Forge, Latchford's, and Kelliher's Mill with its lumber yard and general merchants' store.

Unmarried women earned three pounds, eighteen shillings a week working in offices and shops, considerably less in the knitwear factory in Clash and, God forbid, the laundries, or as domestics for those families who had the wherewithal to pay. When a woman married on a Saturday, she was fired the previous Friday. Such was life in Tralee, a relatively progressive town in the west of Ireland.

The only way out of early marriage, Friday night at the pub, and half a dozen children by the time a man reached the age of thirty, was immigration. And so, beginning in 1959, in ones and twos, the O'Connors boarded various Aer Lingus flights to America, first Keith and John, then Norah and Jimmy. Anne and her husband moved to Boston for eight years and then came home. "There's nothing here that we can't have in Tralee," was her myopic quote. Four more daughters married local men and stayed put. Michael, the last born, twenty-two years younger than Keith, didn't take the plunge until 1980, well after Norah had been sent home in disgrace.

For a while, she'd shared Keith and John's one-bed-room apartment on Beacon Street in the Irish community of Dorchester, sleeping on the couch, cooking and cleaning for all of them and working at what she did best, caring for other people's children. Unlike Jimmy, who came five years later, she didn't bother saving for the just-in-case-it-didn't-work-out ticket home. Boston was home. There was no going back.

She settled in easily. There were enough Tralee natives within three blocks of where she landed to make it comfortable. Kennedy's Dairy, on the corner of Union Square, the meeting place for single Catholics, sold coffee and pastry after Mass on Sundays. Dorchester Avenue, with its import shops, supplied Irish bacon and sausage, Bewley's tea, brown sauce, oats for porridge and Ploughman's Pickle, all the necessaries for a complete pantry. St. Joseph's, the parish church, offered three Masses every Sunday with Father Patrick O'Sullivan, a Tralee man and schoolmate of Norah's brother, Keith, officiating. The O'Sullivans from Ballyard were lace curtain Irish and didn't socialize with the working class O'Connors from Kevin Barry's Villas, but when they met on the street in Tralee, both families were civil, if not friendly.

In America, it was different. Immigration was the bond that equalized the classes. In Boston, Catholics populated the police department, the clergy, construction sites, local politics and, to a degree, organized crime. Not that that meant anything to the illegal O'Connors who wanted nothing more than to keep their heads above water. Keith and John and later Norah spent their first years ducking and diving, greasing a few palms, slapping a few backs and staying put, working and playing music for cash in areas they deemed safe for those who'd outstayed their visitor's visas while waiting for alien cards.

Norah, happy to be away from the laundry and nine children, seven siblings and two fostered in a small council house, worked mornings at the Polish bakery where the fruit loaf, or brack as they called it at home, was as close to the ones her mother bought at Barry's Bakery in Tralee as any she'd sampled.

In the afternoons, she helped Sister Bernadette teach catechism to Catholic second graders who did not attend St. Joseph's parochial school. Father Patrick had recommended her. Sister Bernadette, her hands full with nearly fifty seven-year-olds, welcomed Norah with open arms. Her wages at the bakery and the token amount she earned at the school were enough for her to rent a studio apartment on her own. Unlike the boys, she sent no money home. It wasn't expected. She was only a woman.

It started out so innocently, the handsome parish priest and the young woman from the same town in Ireland. Norah had gone to the ten o'clock service with Keith and John, happy that the Mass was said by one of their own. Not that an O'Sullivan had ever been one of their own, but things were different here in America, and memories weren't always the same when people looked back.

One Sunday after Mass, her brothers walked ahead. She lagged behind to greet the priest.

"How are you, Norah?" he asked, resplendent and secure in his vestments. "You're looking well."

"I'm grand, Father, thank you."

He was politeness itself. "Boston suits you, then?"

"It does." Her eyes sparkled. "It's exciting with so many people and so much to do."

"You don't miss Tralee?"

She shook her head emphatically. "I don't, Father. The choices here are better than anything we could get in Tralee, and the supermarkets have all a person could want. I love that they open every day, even Sunday."

He laughed. "I suppose they do. I never thought of that." Having given her the obligatory minute and a half, he turned away, signaling their contact was over.

"I don't imagine you would," she said, surprising him.

He turned back, this time really looking at her, a slender girl with brown hair, round blue eyes and a mouth bare of lipstick, nothing at all that would jog his memory if he saw her again. And yet, curiosity prompted his question. "Why not?"

She shrugged. "Do priests here in America shop for themselves?"

"Not usually."

"I didn't think so." She tilted her head, her finger on her chin. "I could be wrong, but I don't remember seeing you in any of the shops back home either. I mean, do you even know the price of bread and milk, Father?"

He frowned. The girl was surprisingly impertinent. Surely, she was in her early twenties, and yet she'd reached adulthood completely unaware of the line separating the lay population from the clergy, or maybe she chose not to honor it. Her *cheek* intrigued him. "I can't say that I do," he admitted.

She smiled sunnily, and his breath caught. Did she know, he wondered, how her thin, plain features changed when she smiled?

"The homily was very moving, Father. Do you always say ten o'clock Mass?"

"We mix it up a bit."

"I see." Once again, she smiled her shattering smile. "Have a lovely day, Father."

"I'll see you next week." Again, he turned to leave her.

"Possibly," she replied. "Although I'd like to hear both of you before I decide."

He was truly bewildered. "Decide?"

"On which priest offers the most interesting homily."

He visibly recoiled. "It's Sunday Mass, Norah, not a floor show."

"No, it isn't a floor show, Father," she agreed. "It's an obligation and good thing it is, too, because you wouldn't get so many of us coming around every week if it wasn't. A little showmanship wouldn't hurt the cause." Settling her hat firmly on her head, she walked away.

His lips twitched. What an unusual girl she was, and why wasn't he horrified at her irreverence? After all, a priest had expectations for those in his parish. He counted on their piety, their respect for the Church and the clergy's role, which was to interpret the Bible, the will of God and the sacraments. Where would Catholicism be if its followers began shopping around for a story-telling priest?

He dismissed his question immediately. It wasn't serious enough to give it another thought. More to the point, with the exception of the last few years, he'd lived his entire life in Tralee. How could he have missed Norah O'Connor?

TWELVE

Tralee, Co. Kerry, Ireland

∾ Claire

The following morning, after a full Irish breakfast of eggs, sausage, thick bacon, and black and white pudding—which is nothing like pudding at all but more like two sausage patties, toast and tea, it occurs to Claire that she needs a notebook, one of those small steno pads that fits easily into a handbag. She always keeps a notebook, not a journal or a diary, just a notebook—a place to pen her thoughts in a concrete and somewhat tangible manner.

She remembers, even as a little girl, taking out the notebook and flipping to a page, any page, rereading what she'd written, all lies, of course, or, as she told herself, someone with a great deal of imagination. She wrote about trudging through rain forests, surviving shipwrecks and rescues by fishermen in the Arctic, always a voyage followed by a rescue. Sometimes the words ring with diamond-sharp clarity describing an event or location she has no memory of. On those occasions, she doubted she'd actually written the words herself. But, clearly, she had. Who else could have? Tucking an umbrella into her bag, she makes her way toward the town center. The young woman at the front desk in the hotel assures her it is a brief walk through the park, clearly marked, very lovely and green with a spectacular rose garden.

Despite the gray skies and chilly temperature, her spirits lift. People are pleasant, even the teenagers. They smile and, more often than not, extend a friendly greeting. The park is fabulous. Tall trees border the walking paths, and flowerbeds, in varying degrees of bloom, color the landscape. Older men in wool caps with their collars turned up. Women in coats and scarves walk their dogs beside rosy-cheeked school children in uniforms: the girls in plaid skirts and warm sweaters, the boys in jackets and ties.

She passes a Catholic church, its tall steeple dignified and solemn, nearly hidden behind iron gates, and finds Denny Street and the center of town. To the left is the Tourist Office and museum; to the right is a quaint tearoom, a restaurant, two hotels with menus posted behind glass, and The Bank of Ireland on the corner. She turns right, walks to the end of the street and stops in surprise. The streets of this 800-year-old town bustle with activity. Small cafes offering delicious aromas of freshly baked goods, coffees, lattes, and cappuccino line the streets along with dress shops, pubs, several banks, department stores, a supermarket, an internet café, jewelry and a hardware store.

Claire needs a pocket-sized tablet. Facing her is Eason's, an old-fashioned stationery shop offering books, newspapers, magazines and paper products. The smiling woman stocking the shelves points her in the right direction. She is the only customer. Picking up a newspaper and a map of the town, Claire begins browsing the journals.

The door opens. An attractive dark-haired woman breezes in and immediately strikes up a conversation with the woman at the counter. Pretending to be interested in her search, Claire listens, struggling to understand the odd accent spoken in this part of Ireland. They keep their voices low. Casually, the girl glances in Claire's direction. She looks surprised, then delighted. "Brigid, Mom didn't tell me you were coming home."

For an instant, Claire is startled. The question is clearly directed at her. Then she recalls her conversation with Eamon Malone. She shakes her head. "I'm sorry. You've made a mistake. I'm not Brigid."

"But—" the young woman stops and stares. A crease appears between her eyes. She is not as young as Claire first thought. She waits while the woman looks her fill and then nods and speaks. "Of course. Sorry. It's just that the resemblance is uncanny. But now I see that you're not Brigid. You certainly don't sound like her. American, are you?"

"Yes."

She smiles brightly, artificially, and heads toward the exit without buying anything. "Well, I'm off. Enjoy your holiday."

Claire watches her walk away, this woman who clearly shares her gene pool, and wonders if she will discuss her encounter with Norah. Claire realizes, now, that even if she wanted it, there is no going back. The series of events leading her to answers she's been searching for since she was a teenager has begun to unfold. She should be excited. She wants to feel excitement, but all she feels is dread.

THIRTEEN

Tralee, Co. Kerry, Ireland
~*Norah*

The front door opens and closes. Footsteps stop at the stairs. "Mom," Patricia calls out, "are you home?"

"In the kitchen."

Patricia walks in, flips the switch on the tea kettle and sits at the table across from me. "The strangest thing happened today."

"Oh?" My mind is filled with Eamon. I put aside the news and force myself to pay attention to my daughter's conversation.

"I stopped in at Eason's for some printer paper," she continues. "Did you know that Margaret Cronin got a sales position with RTE? It means she'll have to move to Dublin. I'll miss her dreadfully." She pulls the elastic from her ponytail and shakes out her cloud of dark hair. "Don't you think it's odd that she didn't tell me sooner? She's known for two weeks."

"It doesn't sound all that strange. Maybe she knew you'd be upset." Apparently, she's forgotten the tea. I walk to the cupboard, take out the canister, drop two teabags into the pot and fill it with water from the kettle.

"No, that isn't it at all. Anyway, there was a strange woman in Eason's. Actually, she wasn't strange at all. It was the circumstance that was strange. I thought she was Brigid. She looked exactly like her, or nearly, but she's an American."

My stomach heaves. I force myself to ask the question. "How do you know that?"

"That's the most desperate thing. I spoke to her. I truly thought she was Brigid and called out her name. When she looked directly at me, I knew something wasn't right. Her hair was different, and her clothes were nice, really nice. They didn't look like what Brigid would wear. I was so embarrassed. I'm telling you, if I hadn't just been over to London, I would swear this woman was Brigid. She's enough like her to be her sister."

She probably is. I should say it. It is the perfect opportunity, but I haven't the nerve. I didn't want to be the Norah Malone who gave up her daughter fifty years ago and never looked back. For just a few more minutes, I want to be what everyone thinks I am, everyone except Eamon and Claire Williams.

Patricia reaches for her mobile. "I think I'll call Brigid and tell her."

"Don't do that." My voice is sharp, insistent.

Patricia looks up, surprised. "Why not?"

"Your tea's getting cold, and I'd like to talk with you for a bit."

She drops the phone back into her bag. "All right, Mom. Anything in particular on your mind?"

I look at my child, this lovely young woman with Eamon's dark hair and eyes, this girl who never had a more serious thought in her life other than what to wear to a friend's hen party. Can she possibly be my confidant or understand, even for a minute, what emotions I struggled with nearly fifty years ago when I was alone and desperate in Boston?

FOURTEEN

Boston, Massachusetts, 1963

~*Norah*

Father Patrick stood just outside the door of Sister Bernadette's classroom, where the public-school children met twice a week to practice the catechism necessary for their first communion. His position gave him an unobstructed view of the fifty desks, seventeen of them filled with children whose parents decided that a Catholic school education wasn't as much of a necessity as food or clothing or even a television set for the living room.

Sister Bernadette is busy with the larger group in front of the room. But it isn't the good sister who holds his attention. Patrick watches Norah O'Connor as she repeats the story of Christ's Passion in a language that is both informative and entertaining to the ears of the small group of seven-year-olds gathered around her.

The young woman was a natural with children, but then why wouldn't she be? If Patrick remembered correctly, Norah was from a large family. More than likely, she was expected to care for her siblings whenever her mother produced another child—a healthy responsibility for a young girl, although not unusual. Still, she appeared to take pleasure in her role as teacher, and the children certainly enjoyed having a pretty young girl to lead them. He caught himself. He must not think of Norah O'Connor as pretty or young or even a girl. There was no point to that. Too many priests had met their demise with that way of thinking.

Sister looked up. "Good afternoon, Father. May I help you find something?"

At the sound of the nun's voice, Norah turned and looked at him. Patrick does not return the eye contact. "Not at all, Sister. I'm waiting for Miss O'Connor to finish for the afternoon."

"Actually," Norah spoke up, "I'll have no time this afternoon, Father. I have an errand to run."

The nun stood. "Norah can be spared early if you need her, Father. I'm capable of teaching the entire group. After all," she touched her nose with her handkerchief, "there are only seventeen students in the afternoon."

Sister Bernadette's numbers were higher than those of any other teacher. It was a sore subject for her.

He decided to ignore the implication. "In that case, when you have a chance, Miss O'Connor, I'd like to speak with you before you leave for the day."

Norah turned back to the children. She smiled. "You're all working very hard and doing beautifully. Read the next two pages in your catechism and practice the responses with your parents. I'll see you on Thursday." Closing her book, she straightened the papers on the small desk before standing. Only then did she look directly at him. "I'm ready now, Father."

He noted her shoulders, sharp under the carefully mended collar of her dress, and her hair, clean and shining, nut-brown like the starlings that nest in the bushes near the rectory. What was it about this girl that drew him? Holding the door open for her to precede him, he fell into step beside her. "It's a small matter, really, but a necessary one." He spoke easily, confidently, as if there was no possibility of her refusing him. "A number of our parishioners are elderly and unable to leave their homes to attend Mass. I wonder if you would mind delivering the Eucharist to them on that day after services? It would mean a great deal to them. You would need training, of course, but that won't be a problem."

Norah stopped to stare at him. Was he serious? Retorts formed and collided in her mind, tumbling over each other. She knew from experience that voicing them will get her no more than a reputation for arrogance and temper. She waited a full minute before answering. Wrinkling her forehead, she posed her question. "What will you be doing, Father?"

He looks blank.

Her round blue eyes exude innocence. "I mean, while I'm delivering Communion wafers?"

"I'll be visiting the hospital or answering mail, whatever needs to be done. Sunday isn't a day of rest for a priest."

"Nor is it for me, Father. I assume this position is a voluntary one and that it comes without pay?"

"Yes, unfortunately."

Her eyes flashed. "Father O'Sullivan, do you see before you a woman who has leisure time? Because if you do, I must tell you I already have two jobs and on the one day I don't work I have laundry and cleaning. I'd like to do something with my life that doesn't involve waitressing or domestic labor. For that, I need an education. But it doesn't look like that's going to happen. Time is running out for me, Father. Do you really think I'd jump at the chance to deliver your Eucharist without pay?"

"I never thought"—he stammers—"that is, I didn't think ..."

"No, I don't imagine you did." She turned to walk away.

He reached for her arm, turning her to face him. "I'm sorry, Norah. I didn't mean to offend you. You're wonderful with children. I thought you might be just as skilled with older people. It was thoughtless of me. I apologize."

Dismissing his words, she studied him carefully, the squared-off O'Sullivan chin, the tiny flaw in his left eye, *O'Suileabhain* or one eye, his people were once called, dark-haired, just the right length and neatly cut, straight white teeth and just now a pulse leaping in his left temple. Norah admitted that some women would call him attractive, especially those who overlooked a certain softness. Norah did not consider softness attractive in a man. She remembered noticing early on that the nuns at Presentation Convent, where she attended primary school, always showed favoritism to the O'Sullivans, small things like allowing them to carry notes to the office or go to the toilet when they needed to while the rest of the class had to wait until the tea break. Majella O'Sullivan, the youngest of the brood, was in Norah's class, and when she forgot her homework, there was a gentle admonition to "bring it tomorrow" instead of a stinging slap on the palm in front of everyone. Norah remembered disliking her intensely for years until it dawned on her that Majella had no choice in the matter at all.

FIFTEEN

Tralee, Co. Kerry, Ireland
~*Claire*

Claire hangs up on the fifth ring, just before the voice mail recording picks up. Checking the clock, just to be sure, she counts backwards once again. It's midnight in California, and Martin isn't exactly a night owl. Where is he? Worry knots her stomach.

She pulls back the drapes and looks out the window. It's raining again for the third day in a row. She'd planned to walk the perimeter of Tralee and people watch, familiarizing herself with the streets at the same time. Rain, she decides, is uncomfortable. This isn't a welcome California rain that drops in after months of sunshine, pelts rooftops for twenty-four hours clearing the air and then moves on. This incessant annoying drizzle, certainly not cold but not tropical either, leaves those forced into travel to don coats, their bodies steaming in wet wool, or to chance it without a wrap and, in the case of women, arriving at destinations damp with raccoon smeared eyes and hair plastered against their skulls. Depression tugs at her mood. She didn't travel eight thousand miles to hole up in a hotel room. Reluctantly, she stuffs the umbrella into her bag and looks around for her raincoat.

Suddenly, the phone rings. She grabs it and taps the accept icon.

"Claire?" Martin's voice, as clear as if he were calling from a room down the hall, fills her ear. "Are you all right?"

She opens her mouth, but the words stick in her throat.

"Claire?"

"I'm here, Martin. It's raining," she tells him inanely, knowing he understands she wouldn't call for such a reason.

He makes it easy for her. "How are you holding up?"

"Too soon to tell. I think I inadvertently ran into my half-sister yesterday. Obviously, Norah's child-bearing years span two decades."

"How would you know that?"

"She called Norah mom."

"Wow. You're certainly making progress. Did you make contact with Kevin?"

"Yes. He's not Kevin at all. His name is Eamon, and he's Norah's husband."

"Seriously?"

"He thinks Norah's oldest daughter is my real sister."

"Wouldn't all of them be?"

"He meant we share a father as well." She tries to make her voice as casual as possible. "Norah gave birth to two children with the same man. She kept the younger one. Her name is Brigid."

The silence is loud. Finally, "God, Claire. I'm so sorry."

Claire swallows a sob. "Eamon thinks I should go home. Apparently, Brigid and I are very similar in appearance. He thinks it will cause a problem for Norah."

"It won't cause one for you." He sounds calm, rational and, clearly, on her side. "That's what's important, isn't it? The woman could have answered your letters. She brought whatever might happen on herself."

"Bless you, Martin."

"I miss you, Claire."

"Me, too."

"Hurry home."

"As soon as I can. I promise."

She looks out the window again. This time the rain seems almost golden, and she has an appetite. A bowl of porridge, a slice of thick brown bread and a pot of tea motivates her to brave the weather. Umbrella in tow, she heads toward town and St. John's, the impressive stone church that borders the town park.

Mass has already started. She slips inside and takes a seat at the back. Confessional booths have lights indicating which are filled. Two are vacant. It's been a long time since she confessed her sins. Maybe Norah comes here. Claire allows her imagination to take over. Maybe, a long time ago, she confessed that she was unwed and carrying a child, and that child was Claire. Maybe not, if what Eamon said was true. The Church wasn't exactly welcoming to children born out of wedlock.

Hooking her purse over her shoulder, Claire walks to the empty confessional, steps inside, closes the door behind her and kneels. "Bless me, Father, for I have sinned. It has been," she hesitates, "a very long time since my last confession."

His voice is low and kind. The accent is and yet isn't the one Claire associates with Tralee.

"I won't press you for how long. The important thing is you're here now. How can I help you?"

"I'm not sure you can. I don't know why I'm here except that I wanted someone to talk to."

"That's a beginning, and I'm still here."

Claire swallows. "I'm adopted. My adoptive family is lovely, but for as long as I can remember, I wanted to know about my birth parents, who they were and why I was given up."

"Is that why you're here in Ireland, to find your birth parents?"

"Yes."

She hears his breathing, feels his interest. Finally, he speaks. "We have a long and tragic history here in Ireland when it comes to women who have given up children. I'll be completely honest and say that while I wish you luck, your chances of finding your people are not good. To give away a child and admit to it is shameful and not to be discussed."

"I did find my mother. I wrote her two letters, but she didn't respond. Her husband wrote to me, but he knows nothing. He isn't my father."

"I'm not clear on what you expected. It seems as if you got much of what you want."

"Not at all. I want to know why she gave me up. That's the whole point." Claire stood. "I'm sorry. I should be going. I don't want to monopolize your time."

He is silent for what seems a long time, but when she glances at her watch, it is actually no more than a minute. Finally, he speaks. "This isn't really a spiritual matter, although I understand the emotions that brought you to this place. What you've told me isn't a sin, so I won't be giving you a penance. I'll pray that you find the answers you're looking for and that they will satisfy you. I'll ask you to remember this analogy; until you step into the shoes of your enemy, you cannot know him. These people are not your enemy, but the message is similar. The world was a different place when you were born."

"Thank you for your time. I'll consider that."

"Bless you, my child. Go in peace."

Claire makes the sign of the cross and slips out of the confessional and the church. The rain has stopped, and although the sky is still an ominous gray, people appear on the streets. She turns right at Castle Street, her goal, Kevin Barry's Villas, where Eamon said her mother's family had once lived. With the library as a landmark, she walks past the Presentation Convent where Norah and her siblings attended school, turns left at the Ballymullen Post Office and Garryruth and then right. Minutes later, she is standing directly in front of a corner townhouse, painted white with a black door. The neighborhood is modest and, by today's standards, unbelievably small for a family of twelve. She thinks of her own home and its nearly four thousand square feet and feels no small degree of amazement at the acceptance of yesterday's generation who tolerated the kind of discomfort their children and grandchildren were no longer willing to accept.

A woman peers out the window, sees her and waves. Claire waves back. The front door opens. "Are you home for a spell, Brigid? Will you come in for a cup of tea?"

Claire pulls the collar of her raincoat close around her face. "Sorry, not today," she calls out and hurries on, anxious to leave the street and a deception that is strangely satisfying and yet can have no explanation for anyone.

~

Father Patrick O'Sullivan enters the rectory through the church office and closes the door behind him, sighing with relief. The day is long and cold and devoid of the solitude he needs to rejuvenate his mind and body to cope with the profession he's chosen. He looks forward to a stiff whiskey or two and a plate of whatever Mrs. O'Keeffe, the housekeeper, has left in the refrigerator. Dinner with his family in Ballyard is still five hours away, plenty of time to read, nap and collect himself for that ordeal. All he needs is a bit of time for himself.

A rustle of papers stops him in his tracks. Mrs. Kearns, the office clerk, is straightening files on her desk, something she does in preparation for leaving every day. But it's Sunday. "What are you doing here?" he asks, aware, too late, that his tone is accusatory.

"Just catching up, Father." She is clearly annoyed. "I left a few things unfinished when I was called home early yesterday. I told you I'd be in at some point today."

He rubs his head, forcing a smile he hopes is genuine. "Of course. I'd forgotten. You startled me, that's all. Forgive me?"

She nods. "I'll be leaving now, unless I can get you anything."

"No, thank you. Give my regards to your husband."

"Kieran," she reminds him. "My husband's name is Kieran."

"Of course," he says again. "I'm not particularly good with names."

"You might want to cultivate that skill, Father. After all, you are a priest."

He holds the door open for her. "Good night, Mrs. Kearns."

The rectory would be empty tonight. Father Thomas is on holiday in America, and Father John left after Mass to visit his parents in Newcastle West. The solitude is complete, the fire warm, the whiskey fine on the tongue, burning down his throat, and not another homily due until next Sunday. It crosses his mind, not for the first time, that he has never *really* been suited for the priesthood, at least not the priesthood he's taken on. In the beginning, he entertained the idea of a Vatican post, an influential consultant to the Pope perhaps or something more humble, a financial advisor, wielding control over the vast assets of the Catholic Church. Yet, he'd never advanced beyond the title of Monsignor. His family had been encouraging at first and then demanding and finally unforgiving. Neither had they donated the vast sums necessary for him to receive a summons from Rome.

Patrick leans back in the large, comfortable chair he's come to think of as his own. Not that it is. Nothing is his own, nor has it been since he'd taken holy orders. He thinks of the woman, the American, in the confessional. She unsettled him, triggering memories he's pushed to the edges of his consciousness. It is her voice that disturbs him, not her accent, which is more like a television reporter's than that ghastly Boston dialect it took years for him to understand. It is more her tone, soft and deep, and the inflection of her words. Then, of course, there is the subject of her confession.

The whiskey is taking effect. Her story is sad but hardly unfamiliar. Ireland and Boston, too, are filled with adoptees searching for birth parents and older women seeking the children they've given up. What is it about this woman that eludes him? Damn the whiskey. She reminds him of someone, but his brain is too sloppy to remember who it is. He reaches for the bottle, leans his head back and closes his eyes.

SIXTEEN

Boston, Massachusetts, 1963
≈Norah

Norah peeked through a crack in the blinds and gasped. She stepped back quickly. What was he doing here, ringing her bell as if he was one of the lads who needed a drop of milk for his tea? She stood very still, hoping he would go away. She waited, her heart pounding.

He rang again. Curiosity propelled her forward. With a quick glance at her reflection in the glass covering the picture of Jesus Christ hanging on the wall, she combed the fringe above her eyes with her fingers and opened the door. His back was to her. He looked taller in the unrelieved black cassock. "Hello, Father; how can I help you?"

Turning, he smiled. "Most people ask me in for a cup of tea."

"Most people have probably invited you."

"Am I disturbing you, Norah?"

"You surprised me."

"Shall I go away?"

She sighed. "Tell me why you're here."

"I'm trying to. Will you invite me in?"

She stepped back. "Sorry, Father. Please, come inside. Would you like a cup of tea?" she asked once he was seated on the better of two worn chairs.

"Yes, I would, and something to go with it if you have it."

"Make yourself comfortable," she said, not bothering to veil her sarcasm. "I'll be right back."

In the kitchen, she filled the kettle and cut two pieces of brack from the loaf she'd bought only this morning. Looking critically at her dishes, she decided against the cups and saucers and chose two beakers. If he wanted fancy, he could bother someone else. She was twenty-one years old and alone in Boston with the exception of two brothers who wouldn't know a lace tablecloth from a flannel nightgown.

Norah stayed in the kitchen until the tea finished steeping. Then she poured the steaming liquid into a pot, assembled the milk jug, beakers, brack, teapot and spoons on a tray, and carried it into the sitting room. "I hope you don't take sugar. I'm completely out."

"I'll manage," he replied easily, helping her settle the tray on the small table.

She sat across from him and poured two cups of tea. "So, Father," she began, "what brings you here?"

"The bread is very good. Did you bake it yourself?"

"No. I haven't the time or the interest. I'm not at my best in the kitchen."

"Where are you the best?"

She thought a minute. "I don't know, really. I'm twenty-one years old. I'm sure it will come to me in time."

His eyes were steady on her face. "I'm sure it will. Meanwhile, I have a proposition for you."

Norah's eyes widened. He couldn't have meant what she heard. "Sorry?"

"I'm offering you a job. It pays more than the bakery."

Norah frowned. "How do you know about the bakery?"

"I asked."

"Who told you?"

He sighed. "Does it matter? I need help at the rectory, specifically in the office. Mrs. Kearns is elderly. She would like more time off. I remembered that you said something about wanting an education. This job would allow you time for that."

A tiny vee formed between her eyes. "I don't know how to type."

"I'm not interested in speed as long as you can spell correctly. Can you?"

She nodded. "But, I have no clothing for working in an office."

"Whatever you wear when you teach the children their catechism will be fine."

Her eyes began to sparkle. "An office job," she whispered. "I never imagined."

"Is that a yes?"

She smiled her lovely, natural smile, and once again, he forgot to breathe. "Of course, Father. When shall I begin?"

He thought quickly. The first order of business would be to tell Mrs. Kearns that her services were no longer needed. He wasn't looking forward to that. "Give the bakery a two-week notice," he said. "We should be able to wait that long."

"Why me?" she asked.

Patrick O'Sullivan was conscious of the heat flooding his face. With it came an absurd and dangerous desire to tell this young woman with the round blue eyes exuding nothing but innocence the truth. Quelling the urge, he finished his brack, summoned his most paternal expression and stood. It reminded him of who he was and what he stood for. "You have proven yourself to have an excellent work ethic, Norah. I also know your family. As far as I know, not a one of them is on the dole. You are an excellent example for young Catholic women."

She laughed. "I certainly hope I don't disappoint you, Father, but your criteria is fairly vague, not to mention that, except for the dole part, it applies to nearly all of us who left home for the States. I'm not complaining, mind you, and I appreciate the compliment, if it was one."

"It was. I'll be leaving now." He headed toward the door. "Thank you for the tea and the brack. I'll be in touch."

Outside on the street, he walked quickly, mechanically, toward St. Joseph's Rectory. The meeting hadn't been as satisfying as he hoped it would be. He'd envisioned something more, something personal, a grateful Norah, perhaps, or a reminiscing of the town they'd both hailed from. He was interested in her impressions, in her past life, her interests. He was prepared to reveal slivers of his own background, his reasons for entering the priesthood, for leaving Tralee. Instead, she'd controlled the visit, pleasantly, honestly, but with reservation. Somehow, she managed to remind him of his position, of who he was and had been, and just how far apart they were. A thought, dangerous as it was, leaped fully formed into his mind. He did not want Norah O'Connor to think of him as her parish priest.

SEVENTEEN

Tralee, Co. Kerry, Ireland
~*Norah*

If I could just finish the sweeping, disappear into the house and pretend the bell is broken before Mrs. O'Grady walks up the footpath. But it isn't to be. She's faster than a tomcat after a female in heat, probably all those porter cakes she eats. I take my time finishing off the last of the porch, tap the dirt from the broom and then, finally, make eye contact. "Good morning, Mrs. O'Grady. How are you today?"

"To be completely honest, now, Mrs. Malone, my back has been acting up again, and this dampness doesn't help."

"I'm sorry to hear that. I'd ask you in for a cup of tea, but I'm expecting Brigid to ring, and it's been a while since we've spoken."

Mollie O'Grady narrows her eyes. "As a matter of fact, Norah, Brigid is the reason for my visit."

"Oh?" Is it too much to hope she has some innocuous complaint against Brigid that has nothing to do with Claire Williams?

"I saw her walking yesterday," the woman continues. "It was raining, and I invited her in for tea. She refused without even bothering to come to the door. I've known that girl since before she could walk, and now she can't give me the time of day. What have you to say to that, Norah?"

"I really can't comment. I didn't know Brigid was in town. Perhaps she was running an errand and couldn't stop."

"More likely, she has no use for old friends now that she lives in London."

Norah's fingers were tight on the broom handle. "I doubt that. I'm sure there's a good explanation. Perhaps it wasn't Brigid."

Mollie's hands settle firmly on her hips. "I know Brigid Malone when I see her. Besides, who else would it be?"

Who else, indeed? "Patricia mistook a woman she saw in Eason's for Brigid. Perhaps she has a look-alike."

"That's ridiculous."

I shrug. "Stranger things have happened."

"Such as?"

"Didn't your own Keith O'Grady see his mother fly by the window not two months after you buried her? And, what about Mrs. Little? She said she had a conversation with Mickey Enright a full year after he died."

"Dolly Little has Alzheimer's. Everyone knows that. As for Keith, I don't like to speak ill of my husband, but you know he's full of the drink when he collects his dole."

"Maybe, and maybe not. Whatever the case, I'm sure it will be made clear in due course. Now, Mrs. O'Grady, if you'll excuse me, I've got Eamon's tea to get."

I close the door firmly behind me. My hands tremble, and my cheeks feel feverish. I peek out the window between the sheers. Mollie O'Grady stops near the footpath and waves at someone walking toward her. Dear Lord, I see him now. It's Eamon. She'll pry enough information out of him to fill up the Sunday paper.

Without thinking past the moment, I open the door, my only thought to remove my husband from the greatest gossip outside of Mitchell's Crescent. "Eamon," I call out. "Your tea is getting cold."

Bless him. He tips his cap and continues up the footpath to the door. Inside, he rubs his hands together and looks around the kitchen in surprise. "I thought you said the tea was made."

"Not exactly."

"Why the rush to get me home?"

"She wanted to tell me that Brigid was in Tralee and refused to speak to her."

Eamon sighs. "There will be more of the same, Norah. I told you that Claire is the image of Brigid. Patricia saw it, and now Mollie. What on earth did you tell her?"

"Nothing, really. Gibberish, I suppose. I said that maybe it wasn't Brigid and that she might be a look-alike."

Eamon chuckles. "You have imagination. I'll say that for you. Did she buy it?"

"Not really, at least I don't think so."

His face is sober again, the laugh lines completely absorbed by two deep creases from the corners of his eyes to each side of his mouth. "You must tell the children. They'll find out anyway, and it should come from you."

"Tell them what, Eamon?"

"Whatever story you come to terms with."

I pull ham, cheese and tomatoes from the fridge. "Did you bring the bread and milk home?"

"I did." He pulls those and more from the bag and begins putting them away.

"Would you like your sandwich toasted?"

"Whatever is easier."

I grit my teeth. Eamon is always accommodating,

without demands or strong opinions, except about this, about Claire. I want to shock him. "I don't care about her, you know. I'm not one of those women who pines for the child she gave up, withholding emotionally from everyone else because I gave her away."

Eamon shakes his head and folds the bag without looking at me. "You might believe that, Norah, but it isn't true."

"It is," I insist. "Besides, how would you know?"

This time he does look at me, and his words are sharp and wounding. "You've been withholding from me for a lifetime." With that, he leaves the room. I wait for the familiar sound of Mariam O'Callaghan, Eamon's favorite news station reporter, but it never comes. Instead, I hear his footsteps, heavy on the stairs.

⁓

Next morning, I leave the house early, passing the Ballymullen Post Office and Nancy Miles Pub, closed now, but not yet sold. I walk down the lane, barely registering the ruin of Castle Morris on my right. I turn on the concrete footpath by the river toward The Rose Hotel, the Aquadome and Blennerville, toward the nude statues in the canal. This is my favorite walk, early in the morning when the town is asleep. It is a long walk, an hour each way. The air is crisp and cold, without wind, the best climate for thinking. Bordered by rock, the path narrows here. There are benches for those who have taken on more of a walk than they can manage, but I never use them. My destination is the windmill with its tea and craft shops and the delightful lasagna Kitty O'Shea serves up for early lunch.

I don't meet as many people on my path since the opening of the Wetlands Park. That suits me. I have no interest in the park with its plastic bubbles rolling about on the water or young families rowing among the swans, dangerous creatures when it comes to their nests. The foliage is nice, as is the food in the snack shop, but not today. Today I need solitude.

What I told Eamon was true; I carry no feelings for Claire Williams, no emptiness or unresolved regret. I am ashamed of my part in her conception, ashamed of my gullibility and of the humiliation it brought my family and me. To resurrect that time, to bring the sordidness out in the open, would be like peeling back my skin to expose the sensitive nerve endings beneath. I can't imagine where my mind was that I could have been a participant in any of it.

Keeping the child without keeping the man, even if he wanted me, which he didn't, would have meant banishment from everything I knew and wanted in my life. Once I thought he was worth it. Soon I knew better. That's always the way, isn't it, hindsight and all that?

Looking back, I'm actually one of the lucky ones, rescued when there were still alternatives. In the beginning, when I was desperate and still besotted with lust and imagination, I wanted it to go differently, but now I understand that the way it turned out was a godsend. My child was brought up in America, welcomed and loved. Here, in Tralee, she would have lived a lie like the baby found on the train by the Cochrans who was really their daughter's child, or the Kellys who adopted an orphan nine months after their youngest daughter left for England.

As for women like me, women who hadn't the sense to keep their legs together, women whose mothers already had ten children at home, the laundries run by the church were a terrifying and common alternative. No, Claire Williams was better off having grown up in America, and I'm better off in Tralee with Eamon, a comfortable man with a good heart. I should have answered her letters, warning her away. At least she isn't pounding on my door, demanding to be heard. Clearly, she has sense and a good amount of tact. Maybe it isn't her intent to meet me. She might simply go away now that she's seen Eamon and the town. The thought cheers me. I'll just wait her out. How long can she stay? Certainly not forever.

The snack shop in Blennerville is busy even at this time of the morning. I nod at Kitty and take my usual seat near the door. If I hadn't turned to hang my jumper on the back of the chair, I would have missed her sitting directly behind me at the table by the window. I know her immediately and not just because of her resemblance to Brigid. They are alike, but not as much as I was led to believe. Even though Claire is the older of the two, there is a softness about her that is missing in Brigid. Her features are smaller, more refined, almost delicate. She eats like an American, the fork in her right hand, changing it to her left when using her knife. Even I, who never purchase anything without checking the price, know that Claire Williams's boots are beyond expensive.

I feel faint and slightly dizzy. Breathing is difficult, but I can't turn away. She feels my stare and looks up. Her eyes widen. Suddenly, she is on her feet, moving quickly toward my table.

"Are you ill?" she asks, reaching for me. "Can I help you?"

I try to shake my head, to pull my arm away from her hands, but she is too strong. Then the floor rushes toward me, and for a moment, everything goes black. I'm in terrible pain. The blinding flash on the left side of my head that felt like a bomb exploded inside my brain is gone now, but I can't move either arm. Am I having a heart attack? No. They're not using the paddles. Thank God! It must be something else. I hear everything: the sirens, the panic, the questions, the calm American voice underneath it all. Would she be so calm if she knew who I was? Then I remember Kitty and realize she probably does.

Something covers my nose, and I feel a rush of cool air. I am lifted into a vehicle, and a blanket is tucked in around me. I'm too tired to open my eyes, but I know someone is with me. It's comforting to know I'm not alone. I want Eamon or Brigid or Patricia or James, no, not James. I love my youngest son, but he isn't the least bit comforting. The last time I was ill, he brought me chili and peanuts instead of soup and tea. I definitely do not want James. Surely someone will call my family. I want to sleep, but every time I doze off, someone shakes my arm and shouts into my ear. Rules, always rules. Maybe that's why old people don't fear death, no more rules.

EIGHTEEN

Boston, Massachusetts, 1963

⤳Norah

Father O'Sullivan looked steadily at his housekeeper. Managing to keep his fury tightly controlled, he remained seated while she stood. He spoke slowly, carefully, so she would understand there could be no exceptions. "You prepare lunch every day, Mrs. O'Keeffe, for yourself and for me. Miss O'Connor is employed here. Why on earth would it be an imposition to prepare lunch for her as well?"

"We have a budget, Father. Are we to provide for every worker who services the rectory?" It was a weak argument, and given the heat in her cheeks, she knew it.

"I am well aware of our budget, much more so than anyone else as I am the one who authorizes expenditures and signs the checks. I was only thinking of you," he continued mercilessly, "and how difficult it must be for a Christian woman such as yourself to eat a meal in the presence of someone else who has none."

"Miss O'Connor brings her lunch from home."

"I see." His fingers drummed on the polished wood of his desk. "Would you care to explain to me why you, a housekeeper, should enjoy the benefit of lunch paid for by the diocese while the new office secretary should not?"

She tightened her lips. "No, Father."

He picked up his pen. "I don't either. See that it doesn't happen again. That will be all, Mrs. O'Keeffe."

"Thank you, Father."

"Please, close the door on your way out." He didn't look up until he heard the latch click. Then he sighed, pulled out the bottom drawer of his desk and poured himself a whiskey. That was badly done. He regretted it already. Damn his foolish temper. He had given his housekeeper more than enough to carry into her knitting circle. It was his frustration peaking. Norah O'Connor challenged him. She was prompt, efficient, appropriately dressed and remarkably intelligent for someone whose education didn't go past the age of sixteen. Most of the time, she was polite enough, but she wasn't in the least appreciative of the position she held or what it had taken to be able to offer it to her. Mrs. Kearns wasn't happy about relinquishing her position, and neither was the bishop when she complained to him.

He was unsympathetic when Patrick explained their personality conflict. Fortunately, her filing system was antiquated as well as completely disorganized, the arthritis in her fingers made it difficult to type and her last performance review by his predecessor was not complimentary. That was enough to seal her fate. Norah was hired immediately. She was a quick study when it came to the typewriter, and the flow of paperwork in the office improved overnight. What Patrick objected to, what he did not understand, was that the girl clearly disliked him. He had racked his brain trying to pinpoint when he had offended her, but nothing came to mind. Pride prevented him from coming right out and asking her. Hence, he was in his office at three in the afternoon nursing a glass of whiskey when he should have been at St. Margaret's Hospital visiting the sick.

~

Norah sensed that someone was watching her. Turning quickly, she spied the housekeeper standing in the doorway. "Is there something I can do for you, Mrs. O'Keeffe?"

"Will roast pork and mash be all right for you, Miss O'Connor?"

"Sorry?"

"Father says I should make lunch for you. Is roast pork all right?"

Norah shook her head. "That won't be necessary. I brought my lunch."

"Tomorrow, then. What shall I make for you tomorrow?"

Norah was confused. Why on earth did the woman want to make her lunch? She never had before. "I don't require lunch, Mrs. O'Keeffe. It's lovely of you to offer, but I'm not hungry in the middle of the day. All I have is soup."

The housekeeper hesitated. "If you don't mind, Miss O'Connor, will you please tell Father that you would rather bring your own?"

"I don't understand."

"He is quite insistent that I cook for you."

Norah nearly laughed out loud. Until now, the woman had been downright nasty to her. She wasn't accustomed to having a benefactor and certainly didn't need one. But she would thank him anyway. "Of course," she said.

Norah had just finished typing the last of the letters when she heard him laugh. Looking up, she saw him hovering in the doorway. He looked approachable. She dropped her reserve. "You look like a vampire wondering if your intended prey will be tasty. Do you lurk in doorways often?"

Her smile disarmed him. He straightened and walked into the room. "Long enough to notice that you are a remarkably fast and accurate hunt-and-pecker."

"I'm sorry?"

"Your typing style is unique. Most people use all of their fingers. You use only two."

She stiffened. "Is that a problem?"

"Not at all, just unusual."

Norah relaxed. "Well, that's all right then." She stood, reached for her jersey and pulled it across her shoulders. "I spoke to Mrs. O'Keeffe today," she began.

"Oh?"

"She offered to make a proper lunch for me. I believe I have you to thank for the invitation."

Thrusting his hands into the pockets of his cassock, Patrick cleared his throat. "It was an oversight on her part. I merely clarified her job description."

Norah avoided looking at him. "The thing is, I don't eat my main meal in the middle of the day, and I enjoy a quick walk during my lunch hour. It clears my head. So, while I appreciate the gesture, the current arrangement suits me better."

"I see."

She waited. What on earth was the matter with him? Was he finished? Should she leave? The silence was thick and awkward. Finally, she spoke. "I hope that's all right. I've always been outspoken. My mother complains of it all the time."

"Norah," he interrupted, "have I offended you in some way?"

Surely she couldn't have heard him correctly. "Sorry?"

"Because if I have, it was completely unintentional, and I'd like to explain."

Her chest felt tight. It was hard to breathe around the embarrassment and the delicious, forbidden excitement. "Of course not," she managed. "I can't imagine what brought you to that. Think no more about it." She waved toward the tidy desk with its neatly sharpened pencils in a ceramic cup and tomorrow's mail filed in order of importance. "Everything's done for today, and it's after five, so I really must be going."

He crossed the room and stopped at her desk. "If you could just talk to me like an ordinary person," he pleaded. "Forget Tralee, forget the Church. If you could just think of me as Patrick O'Sullivan, a man without a collar, if you could do that, I think we would manage very well together. Tell me what you're thinking, Norah. Don't be afraid, just tell me."

She was looking at him now, the blue eyes wide and honest. Her voice was a whisper, but he heard every word. "How could I possibly forget, Patrick, that you are a man, with or without your collar?"

He would have reached for her, but he hadn't the nerve, and then she was gone. Suddenly, he was thoroughly, inexplicably happy.

NINETEEN

Tralee, Co. Kerry, Ireland
~*Claire*

The numbness dissipates slowly. Claire's memory of the events over the last hour is completely clear, but the sensation of being involved or even caring is absent. She is an observer, completely in control but dispassionate. The woman could be any one of the twenty thousand residents of Tralee, and Claire's emotions would be the same, nonexistent. The decision to drive in the ambulance seemed appropriate at the time since no one else had witnessed what happened from start to finish. Now she isn't so sure. It could be seen by the family as intruding.

"Claire? What are you doing here?"

She turns quickly. The mild-mannered husband of her birth mother is gone. He looks forbidding. "I was in the snack shop when she sat down beside my table," she explains. "I offered to help without knowing who she was. It wasn't until Kitty O'Shea spoke to the emergency team that I found out. I was the only one who witnessed her symptoms. They asked me to ride in the ambulance and give a statement." She falters. "There was no one else."

"I see." He forms the words, but he seems distracted. "I have a few questions for you, but I must see Norah now and speak to the doctor. Will you wait here until I'm finished?"

A flash of anger replaces her torpor. "I'd rather not. I've already given my statement to the doctor. My being here will only create confusion for your family. If you have any questions, I'll be at my hotel." Outside the doors of the hospital, Claire remembers she left her car at The Rose. She looks around for a taxi, but for the first time since landing in Ireland, there isn't one in sight. Considering her options, she decides not to go back to the hospital lobby. The entire Malone family could be camping there. She pulls out her phone and calls the hotel.

"Oh, not to worry, Mrs. Williams," the woman at the front desk assures her. "Mary McMahon will be finishing up her shift in ten minutes. I'll ring and tell her you're waiting outside the door. She'll bring you back to us in no time. Meanwhile, buy yourself a hot cup of tea. Stand under the awning. A heavy rain is expected. The weather's turned dreadful, hasn't it?"

Two cups of coffee in hand, Claire waits on the bench for her ride. A priest in a black cassock crosses the street, nods briefly and warns her. "It's going to rain soon. Are you waiting for someone?"

"Yes. She'll be here soon."

The priest smiles. "You're American, and you sound familiar. Have I met you before?"

"I've been to church here in Tralee only once. I suppose it might have been you who heard my confession."

He laughs. "Don't worry, I never remember any of my parishioners' confessions."

"I don't know whether to be shocked or relieved."

"Now, I do remember. You're the woman whose confession carried no sin."

Claire nods. "Yes, at least not the part I told you about."

"There's no limit on confessions. The door is always open." He changes the subject. "I hope everything is all right."

"I'm not sure what you mean."

"You were looking for your birth family, and now you're here at the hospital."

"Yes, but everything is fine, at least I hope so. Thanks for asking."

She smiles, and his heart skips a beat. *It can't be. It just can't.* Nine out of ten women of Irish descent have blue eyes, small builds and inquiring minds. His own sisters come to mind. Forcing himself to relax, he nods and walks toward the double doors of the Bon Secours Hospital. They open for him. He turns to look back at her.

A blue Yaris pulls up to the curb, and a young woman in green scrubs with riotous red-brown curls rolls down the window. "Mrs. Williams?"

"Yes."

"I'm Mary McMahon. If you're ready, we'll beat the downpour."

Claire waves at the priest and climbs into the car. She hands over a cup of coffee. "I thought you might need something warm."

Mary's face lights up. She reaches for the coffee. "Excellent idea. Thank you very much. It's been one of those days."

"Do you work at the hospital?"

Mary nods. "I'm an operating room nurse. Sometimes it's wonderful. Today wasn't." She glances at Claire. "You look familiar. Is this your first visit to Tralee?"

Claire looks out the window. "Yes. It's a lovely town. Are you a native?"

"Born and raised. I'm not sure Tralee qualifies as lovely, but the Kerry countryside is among the most beautiful in Ireland. I hope you'll visit the Dingle Peninsula and drive the Ring of Kerry."

"I'd like that. Are there any other sites you would recommend visiting?" Claire listens politely as Mary fills their remaining minutes together with travel information. She knows there will be no memory of the conversation when she steps out of the car. Before long, the streets look familiar again, and with heartfelt thanks, she bids her chauffeur goodbye, unlocks the door to her hotel room and collapses, exhausted, on the bed. Her last thought before sliding into sleep is Martin. After several days with no developments, she finally has something to report.

~

The double ring of the hotel telephone wakes her. Groggily, she sits up, brushes her hair away from her face and reaches for the phone. "Hello?"

"Claire, this is Eamon Malone. It seems I'm under an obligation to you. I wonder if we might speak some time today."

The difference in his tone brushes away the anger she felt at the hospital. She looks at the clock. It's nearly seven. She's not willing to go out again, but she can spare Eamon a few minutes if he'll come to her. "I'll meet you in the hotel bar in half an hour."

Exactly on time, Claire looks around the lobby. Eamon is already there, a pint of Guinness and a glass of white wine in front of him. He's chosen a seat overlooking the canal. She sits across from him. "How is Norah?"

"Stable. We're waiting for test results." He pushes the wine across the table. "I took the liberty of asking your drink preference."

"Thank you." She doesn't touch the wine. "You wanted to see me?"

He nods, looking embarrassed. "I wanted to thank you for acting so quickly when Norah collapsed. The doctors believe it will make all the difference. Did you say you didn't know it was her?"

"Yes, I told you that at the hospital. I didn't know her name until Mrs. O'Shea spoke to the emergency team."

Eamon turns his glass around several times until the silence becomes awkward. Avoiding eye contact, he finally speaks. "I went back to the snack shop to see where the two of you were sitting. She definitely saw you. I'm sure she knew who you were. She had to have known."

Claire waits, fairly sure she knows where this is going.

"She's not strong," he continues. "I believe the shock of seeing you caused her condition."

Claire's voice is clear and steady, without the slightest hint of emotion. "If that's true, I'm sorry, but it's unlikely. Healthy people don't have strokes or heart attacks because something unpleasant, or even shocking, occurs in their lives." Claire leans toward him. "I don't want to make an enemy of you, Eamon, but you won't shame me away. I'm going to have my questions answered before I leave Tralee, and those answers need to make sense. As you're aware, your wife keeps secrets. That's my polite way of calling her a liar. Any sympathy I might have had for a young, unmarried, pregnant girl is long gone due to the dishonest and cowardly way she's treated me. If what happened today is a direct result of my being here, it's completely her fault. If she'd answered my letter and told me the truth, this wouldn't be happening."

He studies her face. "You haven't touched your wine."

"I'm not in a drinking mood."

"You're angry. There's no need. I came to tell you that Brigid will be here tomorrow. I'm going to come right out with it, all of it, and give her your direction. Maybe the two of you can talk to Norah together, if she's up for visitors. Until then, I wish you the best, Mrs. Williams."

~

Claire wakes before dawn and pulls the comforter over her shoulders. Despite the controlled temperature, she's cold. She looks at the clock. It's too early for breakfast, and Ireland sleeps late when the weather is bad. Bringing her legs up into the fetal position, she considers calling Martin. It's only nine o'clock at home. The bricks lining her patio will still hold the warmth of a late afternoon sun; on the ridge, opossums crawl out of drainpipes, a dog barks, crickets chirp, owls perch like silent sentinels on electric poles and night settles over the rooftops like a cloud of soft velvet. Home. Her eyes fill. Martin will be drinking a glass of Rombauer's chardonnay while watching Chris Cuomo on CNN. She aches for the familiar. What is she doing here?

Throwing aside the covers, she climbs out of bed and turns on the shower. The water flows blessedly hot over her shoulders, and slowly, the tight feeling leaves her back and neck. She takes her time bathing and dressing. Outside her window, the discouraging gray sky nearly tempts her to crawl back into bed and write off the day. She regroups. It is nearly seven, the earliest a hot breakfast is served. The morning paper has been slipped under the door. Claire picks it up along with her purse and coat and makes her way downstairs to the empty breakfast room.

Twenty minutes later, the sky is still a forbidding gray, but there is human life about. Claire walks toward Denny Street and the unmistakable aroma of rising yeast. Coffee and teashops open their doors for early business. Trucks shift gears to begin the slow slog through narrow twelfth-century streets. The steeple of St. John's Parish Church pushes through the rain clouds. Claire purposely chooses her direction, following the Town Centre signpost, into the park, past the rosebushes and through the iron gates of the

Catholic Church. The mass schedule begins at 9:00 a.m. It is 7:30 a.m.

The doors are unlocked. She steps inside the church, walks to the middle of the aisle, chooses a pew, kneels on the hassock, closes her eyes and assumes the prayer position. Her mind goes blank. Where to begin? What does she want? What would be a satisfying resolution to this painful journey into her past? Claire opens her eyes. The flickering candles and soft lights illuminating the stained-glass windows distract her. It's cold, very cold. She senses another presence, stands and turns. Golden candlelight smears in the darkness.

The priest she recognizes from the hospital speaks first. "I thought it was you."

"This time, I'm not here for confession."

"Fair enough. Why are you here?"

Claire shrugs. "I'm not sure. I'm at a crossroads, and it seemed the right place to go."

He nods. "Can I help?"

"Possibly."

He stands. "Well, then, follow me. It's cold in here. We'll share a pot of tea in the rectory."

Claire has never been inside a rectory. The sitting room is beautifully furnished with antique chairs facing the licking flames of a large, ornate fireplace. Long windows look down on the town park, and a Persian carpet covers gleaming oak floors. She is surprised at how secular it feels.

He gestures toward the chair nearest the fire. "Please, sit down. The housekeeper isn't in yet, but I make a fairly decent pot of tea. Do you take milk and sugar?"

"Yes, please. But that's all. I had breakfast."

He disappears into the hall, leaving her to sink into the overstuffed chair and hold out her frozen hands to the flames. She closes her eyes, lapping up the comfort.

Minutes later, Claire hears his steps in the hall. He enters carrying a tray complete with teapot, cups and saucers, a milk pitcher and two spoons, no pastry. "You follow directions well."

He looks startled. "I beg your pardon."

She nods at the tray. "No pastries, just tea."

"I hope it's all right. You didn't develop hunger pangs in the few minutes I was gone?"

She laughs. "I'm completely serious. I always feel guilty when I'm offered delicious-looking pastries and I'm not at all hungry."

"That's all right then." He sets the tray on an ottoman and pours two cups of tea, handing her one. "We've never been introduced. I'm Patrick O'Sullivan, pastor of St. John's parish and a native of Tralee. Whom do I have the pleasure of conversing with?"

"Claire Williams, I own a combination café and bakery in Southern California."

He laughs. "Very impressive. No wonder you don't care to sample any of our pastries."

"It isn't that at all. I love the food here. It's just that I'm not a big eater."

"Are you a California native, Mrs. Williams?" His words were casual, but his eyes probed.

"No, I'm a blow in like most Californians."

He waits, but she doesn't elaborate. "Well, then. How can I help you? I remember that you were looking to make contact with your birth mother. Have you had any luck?"

"Yes, I have. But now I'm wondering if I've made a mistake."

"How so?"

Claire shakes her head. "My husband told me I wouldn't be satisfied with just meeting her. He said I would need to know why she gave me up, and if I wasn't happy with the answer, it would hurt more than help."

"Was he right?"

She looks through the windows at the heavy gray sky, the dark trees and empty sidewalks. "I didn't believe him at first, but now things have changed, and I think he may be right." She looks directly at him with those round blue eyes, and his heart sinks.

He clears his throat. "What's changed?"

"Well, first of all, I've met her. Coincidentally, we were at the same small restaurant near the windmill. She fainted. At least I thought she did, but it was actually a small stroke that caused her fall. I was the only one who saw it. There was no one else with her, so I rode in the ambulance to the hospital." She folds her hands and breathes before continuing. "I believe I told you that her husband and I met previously. At first he thought she and I should meet, but then he changed his mind. Apparently, I've caused problems in the family."

"I'm sorry."

"Don't be. I'm thinking of going home. I miss my husband." She laughs. "I miss the sun. But then it will all have been for nothing."

"Have you actually spoken to your birth mother?"

Claire shook her head. "I'd hoped to, but it didn't happen. Her husband told me that I have a younger sister. We're a year apart, and since I've come, I've learned that we share both parents. She won't name my father or the details of how I came to be adopted or why she chose to give me up but keep my younger sister. I believe she's protecting the man who deserted her, but why?"

The silence stretches out between them. Had she shocked him? "Thanks for listening, Father, and for the tea. I really should be going."

"I haven't really helped you. Can you tell me your mother's name?"

She shakes her head and reaches for her coat. "You've been very kind. I just needed to voice my situation to a real person. I *could* tell you her name, but I'd rather not." She stands. "I'll let myself out. I remember the way out."

It is a long time before he finds the motivation to leave his chair. Claire Williams is very like her mother: older, more sophisticated, but just as outspoken, and courageous even. His reckoning has finally come.

TWENTY

Tralee, Co. Kerry, Ireland
~*Norah*

Someone is talking to me. It's hard to open my eyes. I'm very tired, but I feel nothing. The pain in my head and the numbness in my arm are gone. My fingers tingle. I wiggle them. Slowly, slowly, I try to open my eyes. The lids are heavy, but I manage. Brigid sits in a chair near my bed. "Brigid," I manage. My voice is rough and hoarse, but it is still my voice. "What are you doing here? Isn't this desperate?"

"Patricia called me. I flew in today." Her eyes are red. She's been crying. "How are you feeling, Mom?"

"Better. At least I didn't die. I'm not dead, am I?"

Brigid shakes her head. "No, Mom. You're definitely alive."

Eamon steps out of the shadows. "Sleep now, Norah. Brigid will be here when you wake up."

I watch them leave the room. Why is Brigid crying? A nurse comes in and changes one of the bags hanging on a pole behind my bed. Again, I close my eyes. Brigid always was emotional. Usually it turns out to be short-lived.

~

Outside in the hallway, Brigid is staring incredulously at Eamon. "I don't know what to say. Why has she come? What does she want from us?"

"I don't think she wants anything," Eamon replies. "She doesn't look like the kind of woman who needs anything, other than answers." He hesitates. "There's more."

"How do you mean?"

"We've never discussed it, but you know I'm not your father."

Brigid's face freezes. "Why are you bringing that up?"

"You and Claire are very alike. In fact, the resemblance is uncanny. And although your mother refuses to tell me anything, I believe you share a father as well as a mother."

"You can't be serious."

Eamon nods. "I'd like some answers. Perhaps we can help each other."

Brigid closes her eyes, pressing her thumb and forefinger against her lids. "I'm so confused," she admits. "Why are we doing this now? My mother nearly died. Shouldn't we keep her calm?"

"That's one way of looking at it. But will there ever be a better time? You've spent a lifetime resenting her. Don't you think part of the reason is that she hasn't been honest with you?"

Her eyes are open now. "I've thought about that. Something was always missing between us. I could never confide in her. From the time I was small, the lads in school told me you weren't my dad. When I asked her if they were right, she brushed it aside. Norah wasn't exactly a disclosing sort of mother."

"I'd like you to meet with Claire, and then I'd like you to convince your mother to meet with the two of you. She owes it to you both, and, believe it or not, your opinion means a great deal to her, more so than the others."

Brigid chews her already chapped lip. "I don't know. It's difficult to believe this is my own mother we're discussing; a woman pregnant with two love children, the oldest given up and kept a secret for all these years." She stops, unwilling to continue.

"Go on."

"I'm wondering about my father. I have an idea he isn't the most upstanding of men." She shakes her head. "I'm tired. Will she sleep through the night?"

"I'll stay with her. You go home and sort things through in your own mind. Tomorrow will come soon enough. I haven't said anything to the others yet. Norah will have to take care of that."

He watches her walk away from him, down the hall with its shiny linoleum flooring, past a row of closed doors leading to private rooms—a slender, dark-clad woman with more gray in her hair and lines in her face than she should have had. His heart twists. He has a soft spot for Norah's daughter. "Brigid," he calls out.

She turns.

"In case you want to know, Claire is staying at The Rose Hotel."

Nodding, she disappears into the lobby, the door closing silently behind her.

Sighing, Eamon returns to Norah's room and sits in the chair beside her bed. The night will be long and lonely. He misses Norah, his wife, the woman he's shared a lifetime with, the one he thought he knew. But does anyone really know the heart and mind of another? Who was that woman who left home and family for something more that she could only have in that brash new country across the Atlantic? Where had she mustered the courage to leave everything and begin where all was new and confusing and different? Norah's brothers would have been of little help. A girl needed her sisters, her friends, to show her the way. What had it cost her to leave home? More to the point, what was the price of coming back?

TWENTY-ONE

Boston, Massachusetts, 1963

～*Norah*

Closing her eyes and leaning back on her hands, Norah willed herself to clear her mind and soak up the heat of an unusually warm spring day. She can't recall ever feeling this kind of warmth without the slightest hint of a breeze. What a shame to do anything more on a day like today than to pamper slack limbs and work-weary muscles by simply doing nothing at all.

"What are you thinking?" Patrick asked, shifting the weight of his head to a more comfortable position in her lap.

For the mere fraction of a second, she was annoyed. He'd destroyed her mood. She didn't want to think, to answer questions, to slip out of the drugging stupor of warm air, isolation and absolute peace. Despite everything that had happened between them, Norah was never completely comfortable with Patrick. She thought about it often, trying to pinpoint exactly what it was about him that prevented her from being herself. So far, the answer eluded her. Time, she hoped, would end her anxiety. After all, their relationship was forbidden, and even though they slept together often enough, they'd never walked down a street holding hands, eaten in a restaurant, gone to the pictures or spent holidays together with family. The very thought horrified her. She could only imagine her mother's face if Norah told her about Father Patrick O'Sullivan. What his family would say was beyond all imaginings. The two of them had no future, not unless they ran away, and Norah, ever practical, couldn't imagine that either. She knew he was fascinated with her to the point of obsession, but he didn't love her, which made what she had to tell him particularly difficult. Perhaps she didn't love him either. It was hard to tell. Could love exist when it wasn't returned? She didn't think so.

There was no point shying away from it. She drew a deep breath, forcing out the words on her exhale. "Do you ever think about what will happen when someone finds out about us?"

His eyes remained closed, but there was a hint of tension around his mouth that hadn't been there before. "Why do you always do this?"

"Do what?"

"Ruin the mood by bringing up something unpleasant."

"It *will* happen, and you asked what I was thinking. Besides, I want to be prepared."

His eyes were open now. "There is no preparation for something like that."

Could he really be that naïve, a man with his education? "Perhaps that isn't the right choice of words. I should have asked what you'll do when it comes out."

"I haven't thought about it."

She pulled her legs to her chest, dislodging his head. "Think about it, Patrick. The clock is ticking."

He sat up. "What are you saying?"

She kept her voice as bland as possible. "I'm pregnant. The baby is due in six months."

For a long moment, he looked at her. Finally, he spoke. "You've seen a doctor?"

"Yes."

"Why didn't you tell me?"

"I am telling you."

His mouth turned down, something he did when he was impatient. "That's what I liked about you from the beginning, Norah. You don't mince words, and you don't soften the blow."

"Doctors don't mince words either, Patrick. It was quite a blow to me, too."

"Yes. I see that." He looked at his watch. "I should be getting back. Don't worry. There's time. You aren't the first girl this has happened to. I'll make some calls and see what to do."

"It's happened to you, too, Patrick."

His voice sharpened. "What do you want me to say?"

She had nothing to lose. "I hoped you might offer to marry me, and we could raise our child together."

"Good God, Norah, have you forgotten I'm a Catholic priest?"

For the space of a single, brief pause, she waited for him to internalize his words, to understand the hypocrisy of such a claim. When the flush finally rose in his cheeks, she turned and walked up the embankment toward the road.

TWENTY-TWO

Tralee, Co. Kerry, Ireland

~*Claire*

She clings to the phone, her link to sanity, to home, to Martin. "How is Liz managing the café?"

"Surprisingly well," Martin replies. "I haven't checked in with Margot, but she knows what to do if something goes wrong. How are you doing?"

"I'm not sure. I haven't heard from anyone since I left the hospital."

"How much longer are you going to wait?"

Claire hesitates. "What do you think I should do, Martin?"

He laughs. It is warm, supportive laughter. "I can only tell you what I would do, but I don't think that's the answer for you. Why don't you finish it now that you're there? Knock on their door, introduce yourself and tell them what you're looking for."

"Do you really mean that?"

"I know it sounds as if I've come full circle, but what have you got to lose? They can slam the door in your face, and you won't be any worse off than you are now, or you can come away with some answers. Has the woman recovered enough to tolerate visitors?"

"I haven't been told that, either, but I'll find out. Thanks, Martin." She whispers. "I really wish you were here."

"I miss you, Claire. Get some sleep, and I'll call you tomorrow."

Strains of Irish music from the bar filter down the hall. Claire recognizes the tune but can't remember its name. Someone must have come through the firewall exit. Footsteps stop in front of her room. A soft tap on the door follows.

Claire peeks through the peephole. Her eyes widen. With a sense of inevitability, she opens the door.

A woman stares at her. Claire stares back. "Do you know who I am?" the woman asks, her voice breathless and raspy as if she's smoked long and often.

Claire has difficulty finding her voice. She nods and steps aside. "Please, come in," she manages.

Years from now, Claire will not recall the first minutes of that difficult conversation with her sister, only that the tension was thick and heavy like the haze that sits low against Saddleback Mountain after six months and no rain.

Seated across from each other in twin loveseats with a coffee table between them, Brigid speaks first. "I didn't believe them when they told me, but there isn't any doubt, is there?"

"About what?"

"We're sisters, real sisters. My parents are your parents. You must agree."

"It looks that way," Claire begins slowly. "We're very like each other, although I think we would need DNA tests to prove it without a doubt."

"How old are you?"

Claire hesitates. This meeting was becoming very personal very quickly. She glances at the woman who is enough like her for all of Tralee to believe they are the same person. Brigid is clearly anxious and confused. A few short hours ago, she became the recipient of information Claire has known for months. She hears Martin's voice in her head. "*Give her a break.*"

Claire smiles. "I'm forty-eight. How old are you?"

Tears well up in Brigid's eyes. She brushes them away impatiently. "Forty-seven. She didn't wait very long, did she?"

Claire picks up the phone. "We might be here awhile. Would you like a pot of tea or, maybe, a bottle of wine?"

Brigid laughs. "Tea, please. Getting tipsy won't help."

Claire orders tea from room service and then leans back against the couch and summons her warmest smile, determined to ease the situation. "Do you have children?"

Brigid nods. "I do. Three boys, all grown. The oldest lived with my mother for a number of years. I was very young when I had him, and Norah took him in."

"That must have been a relief for you to have your son raised by your mother."

Brigid shrugs. "I suppose I should be more grateful. The thing is, my mom and I didn't exactly get along. Back then, I was a wild child, and if you ask her, she'll say I turned her hair grey. We still have our differences. I know nothing about her past, except that Eamon isn't my father. I knew that as soon as I was old enough to walk to school."

"Was it difficult for you?"

Brigid relaxes against the cushions and sighs. "Ireland was a different place then. It wasn't easy having a mother who wasn't married to my father. We weren't exactly respectable, although my grandparents did their best. I'm the oldest grandchild. My grandda was very popular in town. He was a supervisor at the meat plant, the only Catholic ever promoted to such a post and a tremendous help to families who needed jobs."

A knock on the door signals the tea tray. Claire slips a five euro note into the server's hand and busies herself with the pouring and stirring, willing her hands to remain steady. Every nerve in her body is stretched tightly. Blood pounds in her temple, and hurt sears her throat. Brigid is *not* the oldest grandchild. Claire was born into this family, this bloodline. How could Norah have let them erase her from their lives?

Brigid breaks the silence. "I'm sure your life was very different."

"Why do you say that?"

"I'm looking at you, your clothes, your hair, your skin. You look ten years younger than me."

"I don't agree," Claire replies. "We look enough alike for people to think we're the same person, which makes sense given that we were born a year apart. No one would think you were ten years older."

"Why are you here?"

Claire's expression reveals nothing. "I could ask you the same question."

Brigid reaches into her bag for a handkerchief, crumpling it into her hand without using it. "My mother is in hospital. Eamon said it was serious, so I came home. I assume your reasons are quite different."

Claire knows what she should do. She should reassure this woman that she wants nothing from her or anyone else. She's here to see where her parents were born, where her grandparents are buried. She wants nothing more than to walk down streets where they walked, to see people who share her coloring, her bone structure, to walk into town and imagine herself lingering in shops, gossiping with friends, meeting for tea or cycling to a dance, all the things that might have been hers had she not been given away.

Because she is Claire O'Brian Williams, raised by people who wouldn't cross a street against a light, she will do what is right, but it doesn't keep the bitterness from her voice. "There's a lot to be said for belonging to a large family, a family whose roots go back a long way. It gives you confidence because you aren't alone."

Brigid's eyes widen. "Is that how you think it is with us, all for one and one for all?"

"Isn't it?"

"No. We're nothing alike, and there's no love lost between any of us. Now I know why."

Suddenly Claire feels a great deal of pity for Norah Malone. "Don't blame her too much. It couldn't have been easy back then, with no one to help her. I imagine the shame would have made her desperate. What would you have done if she hadn't taken in your child?"

Brigid shrugs. "Signed up for aid, I suppose."

"Did your boy always know you're his mother?"

Brigid clasps her arms defensively across her chest. "I don't know. I never asked him."

"Did you ever sit down together and tell him."

"No."

Claire is reminded of Lizzie. "But times are different now, aren't they? It's not such a stigma to be an unwed mother?"

Surprised, Brigid looks at her. "It's always a stigma, just not as much of one. My mother is the one who gave me the most grief." Her laugh holds no mirth. "She's turned out to be such a hypocrite. At least I only had one child outside the blanket. She had two."

Claire forms her words carefully. "Maybe we should look at this differently."

"How do you mean?"

"I was christened. My birth certificate says Aoife Christine O'Connor. My adoptive parents told me I wasn't given up until after I was six months old. It's possible Norah intended to keep both of us. Maybe she believed our father, whoever he was, would step up to the plate and marry her. It's also possible that she loved him and believed he loved her as well. If that's the case, Norah is to be pitied, not vilified. She's just a girl who chose the wrong man."

Brigid wipes her nose with her handkerchief. "You're quite nice. I didn't think you would be, but you are. I think you should meet the family. I *want* you to meet the family."

Claire can feel the blood drum in her throat. This is what she came for, what she's wanted ever since Mary and Michael O'Brian sat down on either side of her on their comfortable family room couch and explained that even though she was the child of their heart, she was not the child of their blood. "I can't do that unless Norah agrees."

Brigid's expression is stony. "Don't worry about that. She'll definitely agree."

In a moment of clarity, Claire realizes what she doesn't want. "Don't pressure her, Brigid. I don't want to force Norah into telling all. All I wanted, all I still want, are answers to my questions. I'm here because she didn't reply to my letters. She never thought I'd come here. I believe she's hoping I'll go away and everything will be back the way it was."

"But isn't that really why you came all this way, to meet her, to meet us? She gave you away. Why should what she wants concern you at all?"

Claire recoils. She knows nothing of Norah Malone other than she wanted to escape her past, but surely she doesn't deserve the vitriol in her daughter's voice, not the daughter she chose to keep. "I don't have children," Claire began, "but I imagine it's a difficult job. I can't begin to understand why a woman would give up her child, but I know she was desperate and alone. You're a mother. Surely you agree with that, or don't you?"

Brigid's acquiescence was grudging. "I suppose so."

Claire stood. "I'll be here a while. Why don't we wait until Norah's health has stabilized? Think about it, talk with Eamon and we'll check back with each other later. I don't want to meet your entire family without your mother's permission. It might be very humiliating for her. I *would* like to talk with her. That was my goal in coming here. It still is."

For the first time since she walked through the door, Brigid smiles. "I think I can manage that."

Claire relaxes. "Thank you."

TWENTY-THREE

Tralee, Co. Kerry, Ireland
⤳Norah

"Stop complaining." Brigid sits on the edge of her chair, leans toward my bed and speaks through clenched teeth. "You're actually very lucky, Mom. If Claire hadn't been at the windmill snack shop, you might not be going home tomorrow. In fact, you might even be brain damaged."

"It's Claire, now, is it?"

"That's her name. Although I think the one you gave her is Aoife, Aoife Christine O'Connor."

It isn't fair, really, for Brigid to hear only one side of the story, but I suppose I have it coming. I should have answered the woman's letters, the woman called Claire … my daughter … my firstborn. "Not everything is always black and white, Brigid."

"Really? When I told you about Ronan, it certainly seemed so. You wanted to throw me out of the house."

"That isn't true. I would never have done that. I was angry, I admit, and disappointed, but I took him in. I raised your child. Why aren't you even the slightest bit grateful?"

"You took your pound of flesh. He thinks of himself as *your* child."

"No, Brigid, he doesn't." I change the subject. "Why are you so angry with me? It can't be about Ronan."

"Is it true?" she demands. "Tell me if it's true."

I hear hysteria hovering at the very edge of her voice. Consciously, I, who have spent a lifetime soothing Brigid, pitch my voice to soothe. "Tell me what happened?"

"Dad said you're her mother, and I'm her sister, her *full* sister."

I'm taking too much time to reply. There's plenty to explain, but she shouldn't be the first to have her questions answered.

Her voice is accusing, frustrated. "Why won't you tell me the truth?"

"I'm not accustomed to lying, Brigid. There has been no need, not for years. Which part of the truth do you want?"

"I don't believe you."

I hold my breath. Had she ever sounded so cold? "When have I lied to you?"

"You're lying now. She knows all about you. She has your name, the years you lived in Boston. She has a birth certificate, for fuck's sake."

My reply is automatic, out before I can catch myself. "Don't talk like that."

"Are you serious? Listen to you. You gave away your baby. Who are you to tell me what to do?"

The silence stretches out between us. Finally, I speak. "I can't talk to you when you're like this. I want to go home. I need to think. Please, this is more complicated than you know. I want ... never mind. There are others to consider, others who have been hurt more than you." I close my eyes to stop the tears. "Please go, Brigid."

She threatens me. "I might even invite her to London. She's my sister after all, my full-blood sister. I'm going to find out who my father is and tell the whole bloody truth to everyone, especially Eamon."

"Since when have you called your father, Eamon?"

"You don't really think anyone actually believes he's my father?"

I'm very tired, much too tired for drama. "For once in your life, Brigid, think before you jump." I hear her footsteps as she leaves the room. The door closes behind her. *Claire*. It's a lovely name. But what kind of person goes interfering in other people's lives? What can she want from me? Doesn't she know it's too late?

TWENTY-FOUR

Boston, Massachusetts, 1963

⌇Norah

Blue eyes. We all have blue eyes, as alike as peas in a pod. Norah pulled herself away from the innocuous thought and concentrates on more important things—the shock on Keith's face, the horror on John's.

"You can't be serious," says John. "Not again. What the fuck is the matter with you? Have you no shame?"

Norah blanches. He is right, of course. She is shameless. More than that, she's been stupid. She nods her head. "I am ashamed, but I'm also broke. I haven't been able to work." She stops. There is no point.

Keith's fists clench. "Is it him? That priest?"

"It is."

"I'll kill him," Keith swears. "I don't care if he is a priest."

John laughs bitterly. "He didn't rape her, Keith. She already has one child. Clearly, she was willing."

"He should've known better," Keith insists. "She's barely twenty-two, barely legal."

John was two years younger than his brother and decades more practical. "What do you want from us, Norah?"

"Money," she says bluntly, "until the baby is born and maybe a bit longer. After that, I'll find a job and someone to watch the children. I'll pay you back. You know I'm good for it."

Keith rubs his forehead. "Jesus, Norah. I just got married. I can't support two families and still send money home."

Her heart sinks, but her voice is steady. "What about you, John? Have you money to help me?"

"Some. But that isn't the point, is it?"

She waits.

"How do I know this won't happen a third time? Are you through with him, Norah?"

"He's through with me."

"But what about you? What if he comes back and just wants one for the road, and then another and another? Next year you'll be asking us for more money because you have three children to support?"

Keith frowns. "That's harsh."

"It's the truth. How do we know?"

Norah stands. "If you won't help me, we'll starve. I have nowhere else to go."

"You do," replies John, "and if you're sensible, you'll agree. Will you hear me out?"

"What choice do I have?"

John ignores her question. "I have money enough for you to go home to Tralee. Eamon Malone always asks about you. Play your cards right, and he might find that he needs a wife. He's a good man. If it happens soon enough, no one will even know the child you're carrying isn't his. You must tell him the truth, of course."

Keith voices her unspoken question. "What about Aoife? Can Norah tell him she was married?"

"Too complicated. He'll want to know what happened. Besides, I can't spare enough for another fare, even if it is for a child."

Keith was clearly confused. "What then …?"

The scream began in Norah's brain and left her mouth as a whisper. "No." She can't find her breath. "Please," she gasps. She falls to the floor on her knees.

"What the fuck!" Keith leaps from his chair, slips his arms under his sister's slight body and carries her to the couch. "Will someone please tell me what's happening?"

Her voice is shrill, her words sharp. "He wants me to leave Aoife here, to give her up for adoption."

Keith looks at his brother. "John?"

"It's the only way," John insists. "You can't take her, Keith, and even if you could, the rumors would kill us. I can't either. She's six months old for Christ sake. Who would care for her? Norah can't take her home, pregnant with another child. She'd be a pariah for life. Our parents couldn't lift their heads for the shame of it. Who would marry her?" He shakes his head. "There's nothing else to do except give the child to a family who would offer her a good home."

"There has to be another way," Norah whispers.

John stands, walks to the door and back and then repeats his steps. "There is, but I don't think you'd do it."

"Tell me."

"You can threaten Father Patrick O'Sullivan. Tell him you want support for his children, or you'll go to the bishop."

"Do you really think the bishop would believe me?"

"You wouldn't have to actually tell him. The threat should be enough."

Keith interrupts. "She's right. He'll deny it. Who would believe her?"

"This isn't Tralee," John replies. "Things are a bit more equitable here. They're not so quick to canonize members of the clergy."

Norah's legs regain their strength. She swings them to the floor and stands. "I'm going now. I need to think."

"There isn't a lot of time," John warns. "Think quickly."

TWENTY-FIVE

Tralee, Co. Kerry, Ireland

~*Norah*

Brigid bustles around the kitchen, laying pastries on a silver tray, lining up the teaspoons, and choosing the good china plates, cups and saucers. She hums the melody of a popular song. At least I think it is. Brigid never could carry a tune. It annoys me that she's excited over Claire's visit, as if we never had company before. "You don't have to go to so much trouble," I inform her, disliking the petulance in my tone, unable to change it. "I'm sure she's had tea and sweets before."

"Not here. She's never been here before. You wouldn't want her to think we don't do things as nicely as they do in America."

"I've been to America, and believe me, things are done much nicer here, especially afternoon tea."

Brigid ignores me. "I'm going to leave you alone together, but don't worry, I'll just be upstairs. I want to give her a chance to ask her questions privately."

"There's no need. You're welcome to stay and give me moral support."

Her eyes meet mine. "Morality has nothing to do with any of this. I want you to be completely open with her, and even an audience of one might prevent you from doing that."

She might have a point if the circumstances were just a bit different. It will be impossible to tell Claire Williams the answer to her most important question. "You might as well stay," I tell Brigid. "I'm sure she'll tell you everything anyway."

Brigid's eyebrows, thinner now than when she was a young woman, rise. "We aren't friends, Mom. What makes you think I have more allegiance to her than to you?"

I ignore her question. "I had no idea it would come to this. In my day, five thousand miles meant traveling to a different world. I thought no one would find out. We all did."

"What do you mean, *we?*"

"My brothers. They gave me the money to come home when they found out I was carrying you."

"The uncles *knew* you had a child with another on the way and no husband, and they sent you back here?" Brigid sits down heavily in an armchair.

"I don't think Jimmy knew."

"Good Lord! How could they keep such a secret? Why didn't Jimmy know?"

"Because he hadn't immigrated yet. Like I said, it wasn't like today with your emails and mobiles. He arranged to meet me once, when he visited, but I didn't show up. I was big as a house with Aoife. By the time *you* made your appearance, it was all acceptable. I was married to Eamon."

It's not as hard to tell the truth as I thought it would be. I'd never seen Brigid so attentive. "Eamon knew about you, of course," I continue, "but not about the other child, the one I gave up, this Claire Williams woman."

Brigid sighs, shakes her head and resumes her fussing. For once she is silent, probably taking it all in. Strange how she doesn't ask the obvious. Women can't have babies alone.

~

I watch Claire pour milk into her teacup, bypassing the sugar bowl. She looks younger and prettier than I remember from my brief inspection just before I landed face down on the floor of the Windmill Cafe. Her resemblance to Brigid is remarkable, as if the genes lined up a certain way and then had no time to rearrange themselves before another human needed them. Her voice is different, of course, lower, without accent, like the news anchors from coastal cities, and she has those straight white teeth that all Americans seem to have. I don't feel at all awkward with her, and it shames me. I gave her away and kept her sister. I *should* feel ashamed. "You've caused quite a stir in my family."

"Apparently so," she replies, lifting the cup of tea to her lips.

I expect her to say more, but she is silent, waiting. Better to be right up front with it. "I can't help you."

"I doubt that." She smiles. It lights up her face, and the years roll back. I recognize that smile immediately. It is her father's smile. Why don't I see it in Brigid? But then, when did I last see Brigid smile?

Claire leans forward. "You are the only one who can answer my questions. It won't be difficult. I only have two. By the way, I'm glad that you had such a swift recovery."

I reach for my tea. It's cold, but I drink it anyway. "You don't understand."

"I'll try very hard."

I feel my mouth turn down and settle into the lines that I know look like question marks on my face. "Are you normally this stubborn?"

She tilts her head as if the question deserves serious attention. "You could have avoided all this, you know, if you'd answered my original letter."

"I thought you would go away if I ignored you."

Her cheeks color a lovely pink. "Frankly, that's a bit too much honesty for me. Were you ever kind or even compassionate? Did you ever wonder what became of me?"

Kind? Compassionate? Does this stylish young woman with her cashmere jacket, her suede boots and expensive haircut have any idea what an absurd question she poses? She needs a taste of reality. I swallow my resentment. "What were you doing at twenty years old?"

"I was in college."

"Were you employed while you were in college?"

"Not really, a bit during the summers. My parents paid for my education."

"More than likely they paid for your lodging and food as well. Am I right?"

"Yes."

"Did you have a boyfriend?"

She frowns. "What is your point?"

"I'll get to it in a minute. But first tell me if your relationship with your boyfriend was a platonic one."

Claire looks at me for a long minute. "No. It wasn't."

"Did you have access to birth control, or did you just hope you would be lucky and avoid an unwed pregnancy?"

"Of course, I used birth control."

My fingers ache from clutching the armrests of my wheelchair. I speak softly. "I'd like you to consider this, Claire Williams; what if, instead of going away to college with all your needs provided for, you walked off a plane into a brand new country with fifty dollars in your handbag? You were to sleep on the couch in your brothers' flat, cook, wash and clean for them until you landed a job. When you found that job, you were to save enough money for a ticket home, just in case the venture didn't work out. Just as you're settling in, someone older, who should know better, takes advantage of your youth and inexperience, and for the first time in your life, you begin a sexual relationship. Birth control doesn't exist for the likes of you, so you get pregnant. You believe you are in love. As soon as your pregnancy is obvious, you no longer have a job. You give birth in a hospital, but you are alone. No friends or family visit. No flowers are delivered. You go home alone with your baby. The father of your child shows up occasionally but not regularly. It's the occasionally that changes everything. You get pregnant again, but this time you're desperate because it has become clear that your lover is not in love with you. Eventually, the financial envelopes stop. There is no money to buy food or pay rent. The only help comes from your brothers, who decide to send you home to marry a family friend." I draw a deep breath and fight the anger that threatens to overwhelm me. "He seems tolerant of your condition, but he only knows of one indiscretion. Two children out of wedlock would be difficult for any man to accept. You ask me if I have compassion.

Ireland is not a compassionate country, Claire. At the time, pregnant women were considered loose. Many did their penance in the Magdalene Laundries. Their children were taken away, given up for adoption to couples who couldn't conceive. The man who was your father had connections. He found a Catholic family for you, an intact American family who wanted a baby girl. I couldn't give you that. My offer included shame and finger-pointing. What I wanted was immaterial. I had one way out, and I took it."

She looks at me the entire time, those blue eyes assessing but not, I think, judging.

"I'm very sorry," she says softly. Then she asks the oddest question. "Would you do the same again?"

I won't lie to her. There have been enough lies. "Probably so. It was 1963."

"And if it was today?" she asks. "Women have choices today, and the stigma isn't so great. In fact, there's hardly any at all."

Not wanting to cause further hurt, or reveal why the circumstances were impossible for me, I hesitate for the tick of a heartbeat. Then, conscious of who might be listening upstairs, I speak in a hushed voice. "I wanted to keep you, Claire. I kept you for six months. I wanted both of my children. You can't imagine what it's like to give away your child. I won't speak of it. I won't even think of it. I'm sorry, but when I see you, I don't see my child, the one I gave up. My child was a baby, curly-haired, with fat little hands and chubby—" my voice cracks. "I will not go back there again. Can you understand that?"

She smiles, genuinely this time. "Are there any questions you would like to ask me?"

I shake my head. "You've had a quality life. That's all I need to know."

She leans forward. "Who is my father?"

"I can tell you *about* your father, but life in a small Irish town isn't the same as in America. It would ruin him and me. I can't have that."

She smiles once again, flashing those perfect teeth. "I suppose not. All right. Tell me about my father."

I can't look at her. "What do you want to know?"

"Whatever you remember."

Once again, I am conscious of Brigid listening on the stairs. "He was tall and dark-haired. I suppose some would call him handsome, but I never thought so. He was soft for a man and educated. I had no use for soft, educated men. His family knew no hardship. They had money, you see. He was older than me by eight years."

Claire interrupts. "Where did you meet?"

I don't answer right away, but then I realize that the information Claire wants is harmless. "We knew of each other here in Tralee, but we never spoke until after we both immigrated. It was in Boston that our affair began."

"Why did you immigrate?"

"There was no opportunity for me here. Everyone who could immigrated."

Claire frowns. "But you said my father's family had money. Why did he immigrate?"

"His job, I imagine."

"That doesn't make sense. What did he do?"

I ignore her question. "Nevertheless, it's the way it was. That's all I can tell you."

"It's all you *will* tell me. Still, it's certainly more than I hoped for. Thank you for seeing me."

I watch her walk out the door without tasting the sweets. Brigid will be disappointed. What did she mean when she said it was more than she'd hoped for?

TWENTY-SIX

Tralee, Co. Kerry, Ireland
~*Claire*

The Irish sky clears as Claire pulls into the hotel parking lot and climbs the stairs to the lobby. Tea and pastries are offered every day in the late afternoon, and the rumbling of her stomach reminds Claire that she's eaten nothing since morning. Filling her plate with macaroons and several small, cream-filled eclairs, she accepts the cup of steaming tea offered by a rosy-cheeked girl with blue eyes and very dark hair, clearly a native. Smiling her thanks, Claire heads toward the elevator. Her phone rings just as she reaches the door to her room. It's probably Margot. She was supposed to give Claire an update on the restaurant. Balancing her tea on the dessert plate, she pulls the card from her pocket and waves it in front of the lock. The door opens just as the ringing stops. Abandoning her food on the coffee table, Claire reaches for her phone, scrolls to her recent calls and sighs. The day has been long and difficult, and once again, she has missed Martin. It is early evening in California, a good time to call him. Quickly she touches his name. The familiar ring steadies her.

He answers immediately. "Claire, how are you? How did it go today?"

"I don't really know." Her voice cracks. "The woman, my birth mother, is a cold woman. I can't believe I'm related to her. After nearly fifty years, she's more concerned about what people would think and who it would hurt, primarily my birth father, than she is about what she did to me. I mentioned that she could have answered my letters. She told me she hoped I would just go away."

"Did she tell you who he is? Your birth father?"

"Not in so many words. But he lives in Tralee. I got that much out of her. She also said he was older, by eight years. Apparently, he had connections, which is how he found my adoptive parents."

"Claire, you have her."

"What do you mean?"

"Fifty years ago, Tralee was a small town with a population of 10,000. I looked it up. How many men immigrated to Boston around that time and then went back home? That narrows the field a bit, doesn't it?"

His excitement revives her. "She didn't say when he came back, but he's definitely alive. Tralee isn't as small as it was when Norah was a girl, but that's immaterial. I can research every living male over the age of seventy who returned to the town after living in Boston for fifty years. I'm not looking for a blow-in. I'm looking for a family who's lived here for generations. I have a shot of finding him, don't I?"

Martin laughs, and suddenly the world rights itself again. "You've only been there a few weeks, and you've already picked up the vernacular. What's a blow-in?"

"A newcomer, someone who's only lived here for fifty years or less."

"My God! I'm beginning to see what you're up against. Listen, I'll talk to your dad and see what I can find out about the agency that handled your adoption. Maybe he can shed some light on the people involved. Meanwhile, check on the census, the earliest one after your birth mother was born. Check her siblings, the ones who immigrated. See if any of them are alive. It's entirely possible. If the ones living in Boston are still there, you may have a chance of getting answers from them regarding your birth father. If not, we can check the census for Tralee residents, particularly men five to ten years older who immigrated around the time she did. Then we'll look at the next one and see who is still in Boston and who came back. It'll be tedious, but it's definitely worth a try."

"Thank you, Martin. That would be wonderful. Massachusetts recently opened its adoption files for people searching for their families."

"I know. You told me that a few years ago."

Claire clears her throat. "I didn't think you were paying attention." Their connection goes silent. She knows he's still there. She can hear him breathing.

"I deserve that," he replies, his voice low and humble. "I'm trying to make up for my insensitivity."

"I still love you, insensitive or not, just in case you thought I didn't."

"It never crossed my mind. It never will. I love you, too, Claire."

"I'm going to ask around. I believe the local priest here might be receptive. He was very supportive when I talked to him."

"Sounds good. Goodnight, Claire, and good luck."

"Good night, Martin." Stretching out on the bed, she closes her eyes and smiles. It no longer matters that she hasn't connected with Margot. No news is good news, and Martin is on her side.

TWENTY-SEVEN

Boston, Massachusetts, 1964

Norah

"Are they here?" she asked him.

He nodded. "I'll take the child in. It might be," he hesitated, "easier."

"Easier for who?"

He throws his head back impatiently. "Enough, Norah. We've discussed this a thousand times. There is nothing else to do."

She's been foolish and very careless. She knows that. He'd wanted her, and she him, but love never came up. It wasn't in the picture, certainly not the kind of love she felt for the fair-haired moppet tight in her arms for the last time. Norah could barely breathe through the ache in her chest. She would do anything for this child, throw herself under a bus, work herself ragged, kneel on pebbles until her knees were bloody—

anything, anything if only this whole nightmare could be prevented. She'd dreamed of a different life, far away from all things familiar, where she would live in a one-room flat with an outdoor toilet, the kind her parents had when they first married. She would breathe in hot air, look up at cloudless, blue skies and nod at the friendly brown people who smiled and welcomed her and her blue-eyed baby.

Norah swallowed. The crushing pain devoured her. Pressing her lips against the baby's forehead, she spoke low and fiercely. "Are you sure they're here? I won't have her in an institution, not for a minute."

"Yes," he replied. "They're kind people, Norah. They adopted a little boy three years ago. They want another child, a girl." Patrick reached for the baby. She leaned towards him, arms outstretched.

Norah released her, dropped her head into her arms and sobbed. "Take her," she managed. "Stay with her until she's comfortable with them."

The door closed behind him. She lifted her head and looked around. A lifetime ago, she'd worked in the small office downstairs. She'd never seen the room she was in now, a formal sitting room with plush carpet, expensive chairs and paintings that even she could see were originals. Who were these people who would take her baby? How did he know they were kind? Would they give her another name? Would they keep the small bracelet with her birth name, or would they destroy all evidence of the mother who gave away her child?

Norah stood. She wouldn't have it. She must see them. If they denied her, she would take Aoife back. She would go home to Ireland and manage the nasty comments and rude stares. She remembered the laundries. Would her child eventually be taken anyway? Walking quickly to the door, she opened it, following the sound of voices. The door was ajar. She stepped inside the room and waited.

The woman was holding Aoife. She saw Norah first. Her eyes widened. "Hello," she said. Her husband turned, a tall man with a pleasant Irish face.

Patrick scowled. "Norah, I told you to wait."

"I had to see them," she whispered. "They're taking my baby. I need to hold her one last time."

The woman's fist pressed against her lips. "But, I thought—"

Patrick interrupted. "We agreed, Norah. You haven't the means to support a child."

"But you do," she whispered. "You could support both our children."

The woman gasped and gripped her husband's arm. He closed his hand over hers. His words were calm and measured, his face expressionless. He spoke directly to Norah. "My name is Michael O'Brian." He gestured toward the woman. "This is my wife, Mary. Rest assured, Miss O'Connor, we will be loving parents to your daughter. We aren't wealthy, but we manage well enough to give the little girl a comfortable life. But, if this isn't what you want for her, we will accept your decision. Think carefully. We know this must be incredibly difficult for you."

Patrick's face flushed. "Don't be ridiculous, Norah. Think of the child."

Norah recognized defeat. She'd seen enough of it to last a lifetime. "I just want to hold her one last time."

The woman hesitated and looked up at her husband. He nodded. Reluctantly, she gave up the child to her mother.

"I just wanted to see you," Norah whispered, her fingers twisting in the golden curls, her eyes on the anxious couple. "I wanted to know if you were kind."

Michael O'Brian nodded. "I understand. Take all the time you need."

Norah shook her head and kissed the baby's cheeks. Then she placed her daughter in the woman's arms and wiped the tears from her cheeks. "Take her," she said. "Please, take her now."

Michael walked his wife to the door. "Wait for me in the taxi. I'll only be a minute."

Ignoring the question in her eyes, he waited until she was safely in the car. Then he turned back and spoke gently to Norah. "Thank you, Miss O'Connor. My wife and I will be forever grateful." He reached into his pocket and pulled out a business card. "I'm going to leave my address with you in case you want to contact us."

She took it. "Thank you."

Patrick shook his head. "This isn't the way it's done. Anonymity is the standard with adoptions. There are reasons—"

With shattering speed, Michael O'Brian crossed the room, his fist tight and punishing as it crashed into the younger man's jaw.

Norah swallowed, her voice a terrified whisper. "Did you kill him?"

He watched the priest drop to the floor. "No. He'll have a very sore mouth when he wakes, but he isn't dead." Then he nodded at Norah before following his wife to the waiting taxi.

TWENTY-EIGHT

Tralee, Co. Kerry, Ireland

∼*Norah*

Eamon eats efficiently, sliding his potato-filled fork across the plate for a bite of beef before carrying it to his mouth. He chews, swallows, wipes his lips with a napkin, returns it to his lap and clears his throat before speaking. "You know she's not going away."

"Who?"

"Claire Williams."

I shake my head. "Will we ever get this over with?"

"You're holding all the cards, Norah. Tell her the truth, and she'll have what she came for. You decide." He stands, carries the empty plate to the sink, washes and dries it before placing it in the cupboard.

This has been our routine since the stents in my artery. I no longer cook the meals and clean up afterward. Sometimes, I clear the table. I could do more, but Eamon seems comfortable with our situation. Does it mean anything? Is he so disappointed in me that he no longer wants to assume the normal routines of our marriage? Ridiculous! He's concerned for me, nothing more. "I've already told her everything she needs to know."

He faces me now, his face stern. "Then why is she here?"

My mouth is dry. I wet my lips. "She wants to know who her father is."

"That makes two of us."

"Why?"

"You can't be serious?"

"What if the telling destroys us?"

"Why would it do that?"

"It would. Trust me."

His mouth twists. "I wouldn't be talking about trust just now, Norah."

"You're relentless, Eamon. I had no idea you were so single-minded. We have a marriage, a family, a life. Why can't you let this be?" My voice cracks. "It has nothing to do with us. It was over years ago, before we even knew each other. Why is knowing every detail so important to you? Can't you see how ashamed I am? Do you want everyone to know what *you* did when you were nineteen years old?"

"I already know what you did, Norah. Why are you so determined to keep the *who* you did it with a secret? The girls have a right to know. The man is their father."

"Believe me, he has no interest in bringing up past history."

"How can you possibly know that?"

I have no ready answer. Any more information from me and everything I've tried to hide will come out. I don't think I can bear that. "I just know," I manage to whisper before leaving the room and the cleaning to him.

~

I avoid the streetlamps, although there's no need. The umbrella covers my face, and half the town is in one pub or another without the slightest interest in my comings and goings. Still, I don't want to reply to questions I have no answers for.

St. John's is quiet this time of night. It's Sunday. The day's masses are over, sins have been absolved and all people want is a night out in a pub close enough to home to save the cab fare so they can spend it on one last pint. I climb the porch steps leading to the rectory, step into the light to press the bell and move back again to wait in the shadows. Strangely, I'm not nervous. Minutes pass. I press the bell again.

He answers the door on the second ring. Light shines in his face, temporarily blinding him. "May I help you?" he asks.

"Yes." Again, I move into the light. "Do you remember me, Patrick?"

His eyes widen, and a muscle jumps in his cheek. "Norah." His voice is no more than a whisper. He holds the door open. "Come in."

I follow him inside, through the hallway into a large sitting room. Flames and a single lamp provide all the light in the room. "Please, sit down. Can I get you anything?"

I take the chair facing the flames. "No, thank you. The time for that is long past. I'm sure you know why I'm here."

"Yes. I've been expecting you. Why did you take so long?"

I thought it would still hurt, his dispassionate voice and complete lack of initiative. But I feel nothing for him, not even pity. I begin at the end because both of us are well aware of where we started. "I underestimated Claire Williams. I thought to shame her. She turned the tables on us."

"Why do you say that?"

I had the advantage. The dim light flickered across his face while my own was a dark silhouette. "I told no one about us, not even my husband. I thought to protect myself, and in so doing, I protected you."

"I appreciate that."

I hold up my hand. "Please, don't. It wasn't intentional. I came to tell you I won't do this any longer. Claire wants to know who you are. She wants the circumstances of her adoption. I'm going to tell her. She deserves that."

He frowns. "What will be the point?"

"It will bring her peace, and it will free us, Patrick, all of us. We've lived a lie, my brothers, you and me. I'm here to give you warning. I'll tell Claire who you are, and you won't fare well in the telling. That's all. You don't deserve it, but I want to prepare you."

"I've seen her, Norah. She's had a fine life with good people. What could we have offered her, two people like us, raised the way we were?"

He wants to be held blameless. But it is Claire who will make that decision and possibly Brigid. "We took away her birthright, the right to parents and siblings who share her blood." I stand. "I'm finished now."

"Can I ask you a favor, for what we once had?"

"You're delusional. We had nothing, and you know it. There is no need for us to meet again."

"Do you want me to leave Tralee, go back to America?"

"Do whatever you like. It makes no difference at all."

"This will ruin both of us."

I nod. "Yes. I imagine it will."

TWENTY-NINE

Tralee, Co. Kerry, Ireland
∽*Claire*

Will the rain ever stop? Streetlamps are buttery smears illuminating the wet pavement and moving cars. It can't be more than 6:00 p.m., but the sky is black with clouds. Her head aches, and she feels like she's coming down with a cold. Worse, after her last conversation with Brigid, she's losing interest in her quest. She's met her mother and her sister. She knows why Norah did what she did. Is it really important that she know who her father is when it's clear he has no interest in her or Brigid? She's ready to go home, to warm air and flaming sunsets, drinks on the patio and casual conversation with friends. She misses her husband and her job. Enough is enough. When will this light ever change? Finally, Claire has the light. Opening her umbrella against the slanting storm, she steps out onto the street. She hears a horn, a woman's scream and the screech of brakes. She is conscious of searing pain and then nothing at all, only blessed blackness.

⌒

Dr. Connor Leahy, an attending physician on duty at the Bon Secours Hospital, sits across from the husband of his newly arrived patient and explains as gently and succinctly as possible. "Because your wife was bleeding internally, she was operated on yesterday. It was determined that her spleen and gall bladder were ruptured. These should have been removed."

"Why weren't they?"

"There has been a complication. The RH factor of your wife's blood type is problematic. It's A negative."

Martin, battling exhaustion from forty-eight hours without sleep, leans forward, trying to concentrate. "I don't understand. Why is that a problem?"

"At this time, due to a local emergency and bad weather, we simply don't have enough blood for her surgery."

"Is there another hospital?"

"Both hospitals in Tralee are in the same situation."

Martin frowns. "I don't understand. Is there an alternative?"

Connor Leahy can no longer remember why he'd chosen emergency medicine as his specialty or why he once believed he needed an exciting profession that would keep him interested for the duration of his life. "She needs a donor with an RH negative factor, Mr. Williams. An A negative donor would be a bonus, but we can manage, temporarily, with another blood type as long as the RH is negative. Otherwise, antibodies from a positive blood type will attack your wife's blood cells. She could die. A negative donor would give us time to operate on her while waiting for supplies from Cork. Does your wife have family in Tralee?"

Martin closes his eyes. "I'm not sure."

"Excuse me?"

"Claire was given up for adoption. She's here in Tralee to make contact with her birth mother, who didn't want to be found. My wife was successful, but I'm not sure the meeting was. I don't know where to find this woman."

The doctor looks down at his clipboard. Could matters be any worse? "We've requested blood from Cork. Our roads aren't the greatest. It's safer transporting the blood here than moving your wife there. Meanwhile, Tralee is a small town. If you have the mother's name, she shouldn't be difficult to find. Please understand that the mother might not be an acceptable donor. A child may inherit the RH negative factor from two parents who are carriers but whom themselves have a positive RH factor. If Claire's biological mother has no negative to pass on, Claire's father must either have the RH negative or be a carrier of the RH negative factor. Your wife's best chance is that he will not be a carrier but rather have the same blood type."

"And if neither parent has the negative factor?"

Dr. Leahy sighs. "We'll do the best we can. It's possible to keep people alive for quite a while."

"How long do I have?"

"If you can't find a donor and we continue to have limited resources of her blood type, we need to think about air transportation to Dublin. It's terribly expensive. A licensed physician would be needed to accompany her on a chartered flight. The pilot and crew would need to be paid as well as the doctor and a licensed nurse. It's not ideal, but we can't risk depleting her organs."

Martin stares at him. "I'm very tired and probably missed it, but did you answer my question?"

"No. I'm sorry. Two days, maybe three."

Martin checks his phone for messages and the time of day in California. Then he finds a quiet place in the lobby and places a call to his father-in-law.

Michael O'Brian answers on the first ring. "What's happening?"

"Claire is stable for now, but her blood type is a problem. They're working on it. Meanwhile, it ups her chances if we have a donor. Do you know her birth mother's name?"

"Her maiden name was Norah O'Connor."

"That was almost fifty years ago. What are the chances she hasn't married?"

"Almost none. However, there's an easy way to find out. Go to the nearest parish church and state your case. Tell the secretary or whoever's manning the office that it's a medical emergency. They'll find the woman for you."

"Thanks, Mike."

"There is someone else who might be able to help you. I would contact him myself, but there's no love lost between us. His name is Patrick O'Sullivan. He was instrumental in Claire's adoption." He drew a long breath. "He's also her birth father."

"What?"

The silence on the other end of the phone line is palpable.

"Martin, does Claire know?"

"No. I never told her."

"Why not? You knew how hungry she was for information about her birth parents."

"Patrick O'Sullivan was a Catholic priest. For a long time in my world, a priest's word, his ethics, his righteousness never came into question. By the time the world changed, my silence had gone on too long. I was ashamed. I didn't want Claire to be a part of any of it. I didn't want her to feel ashamed of who she was."

Martin sighs. "Would he still be in Boston?"

"I can find out. Please keep me posted, Martin."

"I will. Meanwhile, I'll go back to my hotel and make some calls."

"May I make a suggestion?"

"Of course."

"Forget the calls. Show up in person and tell your story. The Irish have a reputation for being the friendliest people in the world, but actually, they're very good at small talk and at telling you nothing."

"I'll keep that in mind. I'm also going to pay a visit to Norah O'Connor. Claire's life is on the line. That trumps everything."

"I agree."

"Goodnight, Mike."

THIRTY

Tralee, Co. Kerry, Ireland
⤳Martin

Martin takes the time to shower and shave. He desperately needs sleep, but finding Claire's donor is his first priority.

St. John's is the closest church to the hotel. The weather is wretched, and he has no umbrella. He takes a minute to wipe his feet on the welcome mat and shake the wet from his hair. He rings the bell.

An older woman with the beginnings of osteoporosis opens the door. "May I help you?"

"I hope so. My name is Martin Williams, and I'm looking for a marriage certificate."

She laughs. "We have lots of those. Please come in. My name is Mary Cronin. What's the name on the record?"

"O'Connor, Norah O'Connor."

Mary's eyes widen. "Go away; you aren't serious?"

"Why wouldn't I be?"

"Norah's maiden name is O'Connor, but she's been a Malone for nearly fifty years. More than likely you passed her house on your way here."

"Where would that be?"

"Go back through the park and make a left at the grotto. A few more steps, and you'll be in Kevin Barry's housing estate. It's number 18. Why do you want her?"

He hesitates, then decides her forthright information deserves the same in return. "I believe she may be related to my wife."

Again, Mary laughs. "You Americans. It's a national pastime with you, isn't it? Always looking for your roots."

"I suppose that's true."

She waves him away. "Tell Norah that Mary Cronin said hello."

"I'll do that."

~

Number 18, Kevin Barry's is a small but neat townhouse with steps leading to a black door, a picket fence bordering a concrete yard and a planter box overflowing with purple hydrangeas. Martin knocks on the door.

Norah sees him through the obscure glass, a tall man with hair the color of dark honey, a determined chin and those expensive glasses without frames that only doctors and dentists can afford. Her heart thuds. *Easy, Norah, easy,* she tells herself. *You knew this was coming.* She opens the door. "Hello."

"I'd like to speak with Norah Malone."

"You're doing that now. How can I help you?"

"My name is Martin Williams. May I come in?"

"That depends on what you're looking for."

"Please, Mrs. Malone. My wife, Claire, is in the hospital fighting for her life. She needs a transfusion. Her blood type is rare. She could die."

Norah's face pales. "Come in." She steps aside, allowing Martin to enter. He follows her down the hall past several closed doors into the kitchen. She motions for him to sit down. "Would you like a cup of tea?"

"No, thank you."

She pulls out a chair across from him and sits. "Tell me what happened."

"There was a car accident two days ago. Claire ruptured internal organs. Surgery stopped the internal bleeding, but she needs another operation to have her spleen and gall bladder removed. Her blood type is A negative. The hospital doesn't have enough of her type to operate. Supplies are coming from Cork, but the roads are bad due to the storm. Timing is important." He stops, takes a breath and continues. "Apparently blood from a person with a positive blood type will attack her blood cells." He holds her gaze. "She needs a donor, a parent or a sibling."

Norah sits motionless for a long minute; her eyes linger on the picture of the Virgin Mary over the sink. "I see," she says at last. "Thank you for telling me. My blood type is A, and no one has ever mentioned positive or negative, so I assume I'm one of the positive ones. I'll be tested, of course, if that's what you want. Brigid, Claire's sister, has children, and no mention has ever been made of her being negative either. I doubt if she'll give you any trouble if you want her tested. That leaves one other person, and I can't speak for him." She stands and reaches for her coat.

Martin panics. "I know you must have questions. I'm not a doctor. I don't know the specifics, but if you'll just—"

Norah interrupts. "I understand perfectly. Come with me. The rain has stopped, but you should always take an umbrella."

They walk in silence, Norah, deep in her thoughts and Martin, too exhausted to attempt conversation. He recognizes their route. Once again, he finds himself at the door of St. John's Church. Norah rings the bell. Again, Mary Cronin answers. "Norah, what a surprise."

"Hello, Mary." She steps inside, and Martin follows. "Tell Father O'Sullivan that I'm here with Martin Williams, and we need to see him."

"He's not to be disturbed, Norah. He's working on his homily."

"Tell him the matter is urgent. A woman's life is in danger."

Her eyes widen. "Wait in the sitting room. It's the first door at the end of the hall."

"Thank you, Mary. I know where the sitting room is."

Mary's eyebrows rise. "Oh, very good. There's a tea tray and hot water in the pot. Help yourselves."

Norah ignores the tea and chooses the chair by the fire. "You're probably thinking we're wasting time."

Martin shakes his head. "I've heard the name, Patrick O'Sullivan. Claire's adoptive father said he would have information about the adoption."

"Father O'Sullivan would most definitely know about the adoption. He would know a great deal more than that."

"I was told to look him up."

"Who told you that?"

"Michael O'Brian, her adoptive father."

Norah's eyes light up, and for the first time, she smiles. Martin's breath catches. When she smiles, she is lovely, an older version of Claire.

"I remember him well," she says. "He was a kind man."

"He still is."

"You've made me very happy, Martin. I know it wasn't your intention, but you have."

The door opens, and Father O'Sullivan enters into the room. "Good afternoon, Norah." He nods at Martin. "Mr. Williams. What is the urgent matter that has Mrs. Cronin in a panic?"

Norah's eyes meet Martin's. "Tell him."

Martin stands. He does not extend his hand. "I'll make this quick. My wife is Claire Williams. She was given up for adoption in Boston in 1964. For the last few weeks, she's been here in Tralee trying to make contact with her birth parents. There was an accident. She's in the Bon Secour Hospital with a ruptured spleen and gall bladder. Apparently, she has a rare blood type and needs a donor. Mrs. Malone does not appear to have her blood type. There is no indication that Claire's sister, Brigid, does either." He stops and inhales, a tall man, a good man, a man in love with his wife, superior in every way to the broken priest who stands before him. "You may be the only person who does," Martin continues. "I don't have a handle on the facts, Father, and I'm not here to ask questions or to judge you. Claire is the one who needs answers, but more importantly, she needs to live. Please, come with me to the hospital. Her time is running out."

Patrick O'Sullivan searches the younger man's face. A long minute passes. He looks at Norah, at the serious mouth, the quiet hair and those round blue eyes that, a lifetime ago, first captured his interest. Then, he nods and reaches for his coat. "I'll get the car. Meet me in front."

THIRTY-ONE

Tralee, Co. Kerry, Ireland
~*Norah*

Dr. Leahy is waiting at the nurse's station. "Thank you, Martin, for calling ahead. I'll take Mrs. Malone and Father O'Sullivan to the lab. If you would like to wait with Claire, there's an empty bed in her room. She's been given pain medication and should sleep through the next twenty-four hours, but at least you can get some rest while we figure out what the plan will be."

"Thank you. I'll do that."

The doctor smiles. "Thank *you*. I didn't think there was any chance of you getting as far as you did so soon. I'll wake you as soon as we know."

~

I look away as the needle enters my vein. It is nearly painless, and I watch my blood flow freely through the IV line into the container. I already know I can't help Claire. Not now, and not all those years ago when desperation tore me apart, and I gave my child to strangers with nothing guaranteed other than the word of a man whose only goal was to have it all disappear.

Still, there was Michael O'Brian. Clearly, he was a good man. I saw it in the way he sent his wife ahead with the baby, that she should not experience the ugliness of what would follow. He had been in complete control of his actions. Every move that night had been weighed and calculated. Once I revealed Patrick's relationship to the baby, O'Brian's respect for the priest disappeared. My lapse hadn't been intentional, but it had helped. It was a relief to know I had at least given her up to a man with character. Seeing Patrick on the floor, his mouth bloodied, had changed me. I was no longer the supplicant, and Patrick had become unimportant. Things became clearer after that. Patrick was not solely responsible for everything that had happened; the blame was mine as well.

"How are you feeling?" the phlebotomist asks.

"Not too bad, just a bit tired."

"I'll tape up your arm. You'll need to stay for ten minutes or so, and then you'll be fine to go home."

"I'd like to know the results before I leave."

"Of course. Let me fix you up, and I'll find the doctor."

~

Dr. Leahy pulls up a chair and speaks gently. "You're finished now. Your husband is outside in the lobby waiting to take you home."

"Can you tell me whether Claire has benefited at all?"

"She is being prepped for surgery as we speak. However, your results are just as you said they would be: Your RH factor is positive. You can't be Claire's donor."

"What about Father O'Sullivan?"

The doctor nods. "He's a match. His blood type is the same."

I close my eyes. "Thank you, Dr. Leahy. Thank you very much."

"Thank *you*, Mrs. Malone, and thank Martin Williams and Father O'Sullivan. Because of the three of you, Claire Williams will make a full recovery."

"Do you believe in miracles, Doctor Leahy?"

"I believe in the goodness of people, Mrs. Malone. There's enough there for me."

"What will happen to Father O'Sullivan?"

The doctor shrugs. "That depends on him. Six percent of the population has A negative blood. His relationship with Claire Williams can remain a secret if that's what he wants."

"Do you believe that's what he wants?"

Leahy shrugs again. "He donated anonymously."

"That means she won't know him for who he is."

"If you and Martin say nothing, I suppose that can happen."

I laugh. "If two people know a secret, it doesn't remain a secret for long."

"My thoughts exactly. Do what you believe is right, Mrs. Malone."

Getting to my feet, I hold out my hand. "Thank you. I suppose my donation is anonymous as well."

"Yes. Unless a police report is requested, all blood donations are private. There is nothing for you to worry about."

"I'm not worried. Not anymore. As long as my husband is waiting for me in the lobby, there's no need for worry."

THIRTY-TWO

Tralee, Co. Kerry, Ireland
❧ Claire

Her eyelids feel heavy. Claire struggles to lift them. The room is dim. It must be early morning. She's thirsty, and the flicker of pain in her stomach that woke her gathers strength. Why won't her eyes open?

"Claire?" The voice is familiar. "Are you awake? It's Martin."

This time she succeeds in parting her eyelids. Her husband's face comes into focus. "Martin? Where am I? What are you doing here?"

"There was an accident. You're in the hospital in Tralee. You've had an operation." His voice is gentle, encouraging. "You're going to be fine, but your gall bladder and spleen were removed."

"I hurt. My stomach hurts." She hates the hoarse shaking of her voice.

"I'll tell the nurse to call your doctor."

"No, don't leave. Please, don't leave."

"I'm not leaving, sweetheart," he assures her. "I'll press your call button."

Relieved, Claire nods. She closes her eyes against the pain and waits. Minutes pass. She senses someone else in the room.

A masculine voice speaks softly. "Hello, Claire. I'm Dr. Leahy. I'm going to change your pain medication. Can you open your eyes?"

Claire nods.

"I'm going to show you how to manage your own pain levels, and I need you to see what I'm doing."

She lifts one heavy eyelid and then the other.

Dr. Leahy smiles. "Excellent. This magical little device is called a pain pump." He places it firmly in the center of her palm. "Depress the red button, and the medication will release into your system. Don't wait for your discomfort to become unmanageable. If you're uncomfortable, push the button. We want the medication to overlap so the pain doesn't reach a level you can't tolerate. I'm going to wait here until you feel the medication taking effect. Close your eyes if you want to. I'll just have a chat with your husband."

Gratefully, Claire turns away from his voice. Martin responds, but she is no longer listening for content. It is enough that her husband is in the room, beside the bed, watching her breathe.

~

Three days later, from the west-facing window of her private room at the Ocean View Convalescent Home, Claire watches the gray wall of seawater swell, peak and curl and then, finally, crash on the seaweed-strewn beach. With the Atlantic on one side and the Slieve Mish Mountains on the other, the view is spectacular. The nurses who walk the aisle with her are thoughtful and kind, answering her questions and tempting her appetite with scones and soda bread, homemade in the kitchen. Her gaze settles on Martin. Once again, he is sleeping, his bed a narrow couch, a pillow over his head to block the dazzling sunlight pouring into the room. He sleeps frequently, fading in and out of consciousness, allowing himself these breaks when her attention is taken up with something or someone else. Sometimes, Claire pretends she is sleeping, tacit permission for Martin to relax and nap, a few hours respite from the depressing reality that has become their routine. He has not settled well in Ireland, and Claire feels responsible. He is here because of her. She would go home immediately, but her condition doesn't allow it.

Martin sighs and stretches. She turns toward the wall and closes her eyes.

"Claire?" His voice is soft and tentative. She hopes he will leave the room, have tea in the lobby or walk on the beach, but instead she feels the give of her own mattress. She turns toward him and forces a smile.

"How are you feeling?" he asks.

"Much better."

"Can you manage another walk down to the lobby?"

Her smile fades. "I can if that's what you want to do."

He reaches for her hand. "There's something I have to tell you, and I'm not comfortable waiting any longer."

"My goodness. That sounds ominous."

Martin shakes his head. "It's not ominous at all, or at least it wouldn't be under ordinary circumstances. Your accident has changed my priorities. I think it's changed yours, too."

"That's an understatement. All I want to do is go home and pretend none of this ever happened."

"You feel that way now, but you've come a long way towards finding the details of your story. It needs to play out, Claire, or you'll never be content."

Martin has come a long way as well. She wonders if he might be the one who will never be content. Concentrating on his words, she asks, "What is it that you want to tell me?"

"It's about your adoption."

"Go on."

"Your dad has some information he never told you."

"Why would he do that?"

"I've thought about it." Martin hesitates and then continues. "I really don't think his lapse was intentional. It just never came up until now that you're here, in the middle of it. Small things that weren't important now make sense."

"Boston was the middle of it. *Here* is nothing more than my birth mother's home."

Martin stands and holds out his hand. "Come on, Claire. Let's go to the lobby, sit in those gloriously comfortable armchairs and look at the ocean. Everything seems small and unimportant next to the ocean. Besides, it's good for you."

She laughs and then winces. "Okay. But no more laughing."

"Done."

The lobby, a glass solarium built in a triangular design, features the view and takes advantage of whatever warmth and sunlight are available. Chairs, deep and plush, are arranged in groups of two and three, facing the sea.

Martin hovers over her, tucking in a blanket, positioning the pillow. "Can I get you anything?" he asks yet again.

"Martin." She bites her lip and smiles. "I appreciate what you're doing, but this is temporary. I'm not an invalid. I've had an accident, and I will recover. Please, tell me what you clearly feel will be a tipping point in my life."

He sits, lacing his fingers until the knuckles stand out like half-moons under the skin of his hands. "Before I do, I want to be sure you know that I love you and that nothing in your story will change that. You, me, all of us are the products of two people who gave us certain genes that make us who we are. I'm very grateful for the person you are, Claire; your intelligence, your taste, your interests, your grace, your creative abilities, your food sense, the way you look and think are the results of the two people who created you as well as the two who raised you." He stops. "That's all. Just talk to me, okay? Don't withdraw, and don't overthink."

"You're scaring me."

He shakes his head. "I mean to reassure you."

"Just tell me what you know."

"It's the priest, Patrick O'Sullivan."

She waits, not sure she heard correctly.

Martin knows he's not making sense. He struggles to collect himself. "He's your birth father, Claire. He lives in Tralee now, but he was in Boston when he met Norah. According to your dad, he's the one who arranged for your adoption after he found out Norah was expecting another child, his child. Both of them—I mean—both of you are his children."

"My father knew all this and never told me?" She shakes her head. "I can't believe that."

"Like I said before. It wasn't relevant. Your parents brought you home, and everything that came before ended. They wanted you. They raised you; they considered you their child."

"Who is this priest?"

Martin realizes she hasn't connected the pieces. "Listen to me. You know him. It's Father Patrick O'Sullivan from St. John's Church."

He knows the instant understanding comes. Her jaw clenches, and she stares at him, willing him to take it back, to say he's mistaken, that it didn't happen. "Are you sure?"

Martin nods.

"He told me he served in Boston. He said he didn't know Norah."

"He lied. That's not the worst of his sins."

"He lied?"

"Yes."

Claire turns her head to face the sea. "How did you come by your information?"

"You needed a donor for your blood type, which happens to be rare. Did you know that?"

"Yes."

"Why didn't you ever tell me that?"

"It didn't come up. We weren't going to have children. What difference does it make? It's irrelevant."

"No, Claire. It isn't. It's the reason you needed a donor. Norah and Brigid were tested. They aren't a match. Your dad told me that a priest by the name of Patrick O'Sullivan was responsible for your adoption.

Then he told me he was a great deal more than that. I found Norah, and we went to confront him. He didn't deny anything. In fact, to his credit, he didn't waste any time getting to the hospital. He's your donor, and he's your father."

"Are you saying that no one else in the entire town of Tralee has my blood type?"

Martin's impatience peaks. "What difference does that make? I'm saying that, given the timing, I had no choice but to ask your birth father to donate blood for your surgery. This isn't Walter Reed. I didn't have the luxury of being selective."

Somewhere outside the window, seagulls chirp, waves crash against the shore. In the lobby, soothing music filters through the sound system. Yesterday, Claire asked a nurse what the small brown birds nesting in the outside cornices were called. She can't remember what the woman told her. Today, there was oatmeal for breakfast—Irish oatmeal with raisins and cream and thin triangles of white toast, delicious. She is very aware of Martin sitting beside her. Martin, her husband, whose normal parents, now deceased, had never done anything shocking in their entire lives.

Her voice is low, the words unsteady. "I'm sorry, Martin. Of course, you didn't. This is a lot to take in. Norah O'Connor and a priest, *a priest*, are my birth parents. I can't—" she stops. "I don't want to think about it. I want to go home and never, ever come back here."

"That can happen."

She wants more from him, some kind of pronouncement that will convince her that everything will be the same as it once was. She will go home and resume managing her restaurant, writing her cooking columns, creating recipes in her gourmet kitchen with its wide windows and Wolfe range. She will have nothing more to do with these people whose genes she carries. Hers was an out-of-control accident of birth that she will never mention again. First, she needs to be sure Martin is on board. "When can we go home?"

"You have unfinished business. We're here now. You came here to find out why you were given up. The opportunity may not come again."

"I told you. It doesn't matter. My priorities have changed. Besides, I already know the answer to that."

"I doubt that."

"Why are you doing this? You can't want to be here any longer than I do."

He takes her hands in both of his. "We've been married a long time. I know you. No matter what the fallout is from the truth, you'll handle it. You won't be satisfied sweeping it all under the carpet. Let's finish this, accept the consequences, and go home."

"I don't think I can face him."

"He should be feeling that way, not you."

"I told him things in the confessional. He must have known who I was. I can't remember if I actually mentioned names." She pulls her hands away and covers her face. "It's humiliating."

"Claire, if seeing him again bothers you that much, you don't have to, but I believe you'll get a story much closer to the truth if you speak with both of your parents."

"Maybe they won't see me."

Martin's mouth tightens. "They will see you, and they'll tell you what happened. Both Norah and Patrick O'Sullivan were shaken by the events of the last two weeks. They'll want to come clean."

Claire closes her eyes. "Let me think about it."

THIRTY-THREE

Tralee, Co. Kerry, Ireland
⤳Norah

My hands shake as I arrange the lemon scones, Eamon's favorite, on the tray. The teapot was my mother's, bluebells and daffodils on a white background. She gave it to me just before she died. "You're my oldest daughter," she said. "Use it, enjoy it and don't worry if you break it." I honor her wishes. So far, so good.

Eamon will think we're celebrating, and, in a way, we are. I pour milk into the pitcher, pick up the tray and carry it into the sitting room where he is watching the news.

He looks up, reaches for the remote and turns off the television. "Is this a special occasion?"

I can feel the red rise in my cheeks. "Why do you ask?"

"It isn't every day that we have tea together."

"I'm thinking that maybe, from now on, we should. How do you feel about that?"

He smiles, stands and reaches for the tray, setting it on the small coffee table and sits down again. "I think it's a grand idea." He pats the space beside him.

I sit close enough for our knees to touch. "I have something to tell you," I confess, pouring him a cup of tea. "It's about Boston."

He nods. "I'm listening."

"It's difficult for me, Eamon, because I was young and naïve and very, very stupid, and because I'd never been away from home, and I suppose, because I was alone."

"What about your brothers?"

I stop for a minute and attempt to explain why they did what they did. There really was no excuse. I don't know them anymore. We haven't spoken in fifty years. I shake my head. "They didn't care about me. They were too busy looking out for themselves. People think that when you come from a large family that you're close, but it wasn't that way for us. I was the oldest girl and the childminder, and when I came to Boston and lived with my brothers, I cooked and cleaned and shopped and worked. I couldn't wait to move into a place of my own. It took me a long time to earn enough to rent a small flat. I loved it. I'd never even had a room of my own before. I felt powerful, as if I could do anything."

I sip my tea, lost in memory of those early days. "That was my mistake." I look directly at him. "This part is very hard, Eamon. You'll be shocked because it's completely out of character for me."

He reaches over and takes my hand. "Try me."

I cling to his hand and take a deep breath. "I met Patrick O'Sullivan on my very first Sunday in Boston."

"Father Patrick O'Sullivan of Ballard?"

"Yes." I can't look at him. My voice is a mere whisper. "Don't judge me, Eamon. I don't know what came over me." I speak quickly now, hurrying to get the worst part over with. "I must have flirted with him because he was interested in me from the beginning. I taught catechism at the church school, and he offered me an office job in the rectory. That was when it started. I had my own flat, and he came over two or three times a week. It wasn't long before I was carrying Aoife. He gave me money at first, but he wasn't as interested once I had the baby. Still, I got pregnant again with Brigid. Then he stopped coming, and there was no more money. I asked my brothers for help, but they refused. John said I had no choice, that I should put Aoife up for adoption and come home. He said you would want me even though I was pregnant."

This was the cue for Eamon to reassure me that he did want me despite my pregnancy, but he didn't. He said nothing at all.

I was looking at him now. I wanted him to understand how lost I was, how miserable. "I almost couldn't go through with it. Patrick arranged for the adoption, but I didn't want it. Aoife was a baby, just six months old, and I loved her so much, Eamon. I wanted to keep her despite the shame I would bring my family and my fear of the laundries. I would have if I hadn't met the people who adopted her. They were lovely and well off. They had adopted a little boy three years before. I knew Aoife's life would be a much better one than she would have with me. She would have a true family and never know the shame of a mother who wasn't married. The man, Michael O'Brian, gave me his card in case I needed anything, and then he did something I'll never forget. He punched Patrick in the face and left him there in the rectory on the floor. Then I came home to you."

Eamon opens his mouth and closes it again without speaking. Finally he stands, rubs his chin and clenches his fists. He begins pacing the room. Back and forth, back and forth. Minutes tick by before he stops, places both hands on the sideboard, his back to me. The silence between us is long and terrifying.

I watch him until I can't manage any longer. "Eamon, I don't blame you for hating me. Can you ever forgive me? Because if you can't, I'll understand. Please believe me when I tell you I haven't spoken to or heard from Patrick O'Sullivan in fifty years, not until he showed up at Mass a few weeks ago. Eamon, please speak to me."

Finally, he turns to me. His cheeks are wet. "I don't hate you, Norah. I love you. I've always loved you. To think you held this inside for nearly fifty years, never speaking of it, or of the child who was taken from you, of the abuse you accepted at the hands of a so-called Catholic priest. You were a child, an innocent child, and he took terrible advantage of you." Eamon was pacing again, his face red, eyes spilling over with rage. "I should kill him. It would give me great pleasure to kill him, but then he would have destroyed us, our children and grandchildren."

I'm shocked. Eamon is a gentle man, incapable of harming anyone. "It happened long ago. It's over now."

"Is it? Then why don't you go to St. John's Mass anymore? You lost your first daughter, and your relationship with Brigid isn't a good one. You've been unable to grieve for fifty years, and now he's back, right here in our own parish, saying Mass and hearing confessions as if he was pure as the driven snow. What kind of a man does this?"

My reply is blunt. "More than we know. The Catholic church has had a sullied reputation for quite some time now."

"I can't let this go. You're my wife. He's got to make amends."

My feet feel heavy. I want to touch Eamon, to ease his distress, but I can't move. "Eamon, please, I don't want people knowing. I wasn't an innocent victim. You know what this town is like. I made a terrible mistake, and I've paid for it. But it's finished. You and I never would have married if it had turned out differently. My family would have disowned me. I could never have come back to Tralee. Please don't do anything that would change our lives."

His smile is sad and tired. "You're not to worry, Norah. You won't be involved at all other than telling Brigid the truth. I will, however, pay Father O'Sullivan a visit."

My phone conversation with Brigid is surprisingly easy. She takes the news about Patrick with a composure I didn't know she was capable of. I suppose it helps that she is away in London and never knew the O'Sullivans. Most likely, her lack of interest in the Catholic faith has something to do with it. The younger generation has seen the crimes of the clergy slapped all over the news for the last twenty years. There is no expectation that nuns and priests lead perfect lives.

I reassure her that she can do as she pleases with the information. I won't tell Patricia and James. It isn't their story. They were born in Tralee, and Eamon is their father.

Claire is an odd sort of complication. I don't know that she'll ever come back to Ireland. I doubt she wants to pursue a relationship with me. I've done too much damage there. Something happened when I gave her up, not immediately, but later. At first, I imagined that she would be restored to me, that I could show up at the O'Brian household and claim her again, no questions asked, no resistance. It wasn't until after I had Brigid that I realized the loss of my first child was permanent, just the same as if she had died. Claire is a stranger, an American, a woman raised in an affluent home—Michael and Mary O'Brian's child, not mine. At least I gave her that. We share nothing; not even our blood types are the same. It is Patrick who saved her life. To his credit, his decision to do so was immediate, without hesitation. Brigid is the one who sustained the most damage, never fitting in with the others, not knowing who her father was, running off to London and never coming home, not permanently anyway, and now, finding she has a sister only to lose her again. What can I do about Brigid?

THIRTY-FOUR

Tralee, Co. Kerry, Ireland
⁓Patrick

Patrick knows that small towns cannot hide secrets for long. It doesn't matter. His parents are dead, his siblings old. He has no one to answer to but himself ... and Norah. Perhaps it's time to retire. He is alone in the rectory. The fire is warm like the Irish whiskey that numbs his tongue as it makes its way down his throat. No visiting priests or even the housekeeper mar the perfect stillness of the evening. He closes his eyes and imagines what life would be like in Italy, not Rome or Florence, but in a small mountain town, Sienna, perhaps, or Assisi, where the days are lazy and long and expectations few. He imagines olive trees and vineyards and oranges in bowls of brightly colored pottery, narrow streets and long, crunchy bread loaves filling bakery windows, and sand-colored buildings with blinds that block the sun.

He is nearly asleep when he hears the knocking. Fumbling with his phone, he checks the time; a bit late for a visit but not out of the question. The knocking becomes more persistent. Patrick flips on the porch lights and opens the door. His eyes widen. "Hello, Eamon. This is a surprise. How can I help you?"

Eamon steps around him into the room. "This won't take long. You remember my wife, Norah, don't you, Patrick?"

He notices Eamon doesn't address him by his title. "I do."

Eamon stares him down. "She told me the part you played while she was living in America. She's hidden the sordid details of that story for nearly fifty years. It cost her a great deal to come out with them."

"I suppose she told you I was to blame."

Eamon's control broke. "You *are* to blame. You're a Catholic priest, a person of authority. You gave her a job. She was young and alone. You took advantage of her."

Patrick sighs. "As you said, it was a long time ago. I have a great many regrets. Norah is one of them."

"That's all you have to say?"

"What would you have me do, Eamon?"

"Norah and I have a family, children and grandchildren. You show up here without a care in the world, as if it's all up to you, as if seeing you here in Tralee after what she went through means nothing? Norah shouldn't have to see you every Sunday. She shouldn't have to see you again. You're of an age to take redundancy. I want you out of here, now. Go back to America or wherever else they'll have you, but not here and not in Ireland. You don't deserve to come home."

"And if I don't do as you ask?"

"Those in high places will know. I'm not such a fool as to think you'll be censured. God knows enough of you have gone down the same path. The likes of you get moved around, but that's the end of it. No recriminations, no penance, nothing more than a slap on the wrist. But I'm a familiar face here in Tralee. I have a reputation for saying it like it is. If I spread the word, you won't be accepted here any longer. People will know you for a hypocrite. They'll cut you to your face. You'll bring shame to your family."

"What about Norah's shame? Aren't you concerned about what she'll face if everyone knows about her past?"

Eamon ignores his question. "You have two weeks, no more. We won't be speaking again whatever you decide." He opens the door and walks down the footpath.

"It all happened before she married you, Eamon," Patrick calls out. "We were two consenting adults."

Eamon turns. "And what of the children you tossed away? Were they consenting adults, too?"

Patrick shakes his head and watches Eamon Malone disappear into the night. "It appears I need an escape plan," he says to himself.

THIRTY-FIVE

Tralee, Co. Kerry, Ireland
∼ *Claire*

"I can't find my gray infinity scarf, the soft one. Have you seen it?"

Martin shakes his head. "Are you sure you brought it?"

"I can't remember now." She frowns. "In fact, I can't remember a lot of things lately."

Martin looks up from his laptop. "You've been through major surgery in a foreign country. Give yourself some time."

"I suppose. Have you found us a flight?"

"There's one leaving on Thursday that will take us into Orange County. We'll have two stops, though. I'd really like to get it down to one."

Her voice cracks. "Thursday is four days away."

Martin walks around the bed and takes Claire into his arms. "I'll keep trying."

She buries her face in his shoulder. "I'm sorry, Martin. I'm a witch. It must seem like I'm always complaining. I have no one to blame but myself for being here in this condition."

He kisses the top of her head. "I think you have some unfinished business, sweetheart."

"I've gotten all that I can from Norah. I understand why she did what she did. Starvation and shame are strong motivations. She's only human. I accept that she wanted to keep me and why she didn't answer my letters, although I don't agree with her."

"Norah isn't your unfinished business."

Claire pulls away. "You mean the priest."

"Yes."

"I doubt he has anything to say that will make a difference. He's selfish and completely lacking in compassion. What kind of man gives away his children?"

"A terrified one born into a completely different world than the one we grew up in. The church was all he knew. *Excommunicated Roman Catholic Priest* isn't exactly a gold star on a resume."

"Are you defending him?"

"Not at all."

"Then why do you want me to see him?"

Martin sits on the bed and pulls her down beside him. "I think you'll get satisfaction from confronting him. I want him to know the kind of person you are: educated, intelligent, and sophisticated. He missed out. My guess is, in his limited scope, he didn't think Norah O'Connor could produce a child like you. There's an odd sort of caste system here. Most likely, it comes from centuries of English occupation. I would very much like Patrick O'Sullivan to admit he's ashamed of the way he treated you."

Claire looks out the window. They are quiet for a long time. Finally, she takes his hand. "Will you go with me?" she asks.

"Yes, and if you decide to speak with him privately, I'll wait for you outside."

~

Claire pulls on her puffy coat and hiking boots, gathers her hair and twists it into a bun, securing it with a clip. "Are you ready?" she asks.

Martin swallows the rest of his coffee, gathers the rental car keys and the hotel card and nods. "Let's go."

In the car, he turns toward her. "Are you sure about this? We don't know much about him."

"I'll be all right. There's a parking lot right on the beach. I'll make sure he knows you're there waiting for me. Besides, there's no indication he's unstable, and he did donate his blood to keep me alive. I'm no threat to him."

"I'll give you the key fob. Sound the alarm if you need me."

Claire nods and looks out the window at the cold gray-white of the sky. "I'll be looking for a delicious lunch in a cozy pub when I'm finished. That seafood chowder place is calling me."

Martin grins. "Great minds."

The road to Derrymore Strand is no more than a rutted, narrow lane with tall, reed-like bushes maintaining the privacy of the few houses hiding behind them. Martin pulls into the parking lot where a single car is positioned to take advantage of the view. Immediately, the door opens, and Father O'Sullivan, in slacks and a thick parka, steps out. He waits for Martin to park and hold the door for Claire. They walk toward him, her hand in his.

Martin nods. "Father O'Sullivan."

"Good morning, Martin." He smiles at Claire. "How are you feeling?"

"Still a little wobbly, but improving every day. I believe I owe you for that."

Her voice is unusual. He first noticed it during their conversation in the rectory. It reminded him of a quote he couldn't recall. He remembers it now, from Shakespeare's King Lear; *Her voice was ever low, gentle and soft, an excellent thing in woman.* "The tide is out. Would you care to walk?" he asks her. "I promise not to tire you out."

"Yes. Let's do that."

Martin squeezes her hand. "I'll wait in the car."

She nods, slips both hands into her pockets and moves slowly up the strand beside the priest.

"What can I do for you, Claire?"

She answers immediately as if she expected the question. "You can tell me the truth even if it makes you look self-serving. I want to know how you, a Catholic priest, could maintain a relationship with a woman for two years, give her children and then abandon them?"

He looks up at the sky. "I have no excuse other than I wanted to continue as a Catholic priest."

"There are Catholic priests who continue to support their children."

He nods. "Yes, but they live a lie. I couldn't do that."

She stares at him. "Are you serious?"

"Very much so. I confessed all of it and was forgiven. My penance was to find homes for you and the unborn child and then to walk away, forever."

"I was six months old." Her voice cracks. "How could you give me away after knowing me for six months?"

"I knew you were too young to remember Norah and me, and the life you would have with your adoptive parents would be far superior to the one Norah could give you."

"What about her pain?"

He stops walking and looks at her. "I'm trying to explain to you, objectively. I committed a terrible wrong. I accept responsibility for that. But Norah is responsible, too. She made choices as well, and one of them was the decision to keep her second child, come back to Ireland, and marry Eamon Malone. Yes, she suffered, but you didn't."

"Brigid suffered. She knew Eamon wasn't her father. Everyone knew."

"That was Norah's fault."

"How so?"

"Apparently, according to my sisters and the gossip mill, she had an opportunity to go to England with her husband. Instead, she chose to stay in Tralee, two doors down from her parents and an entire town who knew she was pregnant before she was married. I'll take responsibility for you but not for Norah and her role in Brigid's suffering. This is rural Ireland. She was a grown woman who knew the rules and made no move to make it easier for her child. Our relationship was consensual on both sides, Claire. The O'Brians would have taken Brigid as well. She would have had a family who valued education and accomplishment. Look at what you've done. I looked you up. Do you really believe you would have graduated from college, attended a prestigious cooking school and opened your own successful business if Norah O'Connor had raised you here in Tralee? Do you think you would have had a mother who read to you as a child or even one who owned a book outside of the Bible? Would she have encouraged your dreams?" He shakes his head. "The answer is no. More likely, she would have demanded that you find a job in the local factory and help support the family. Our generation accepted the status quo. Catholics did not aspire to professional occupations. Thankfully, that's changed with the generation that followed, but not soon enough for you or Brigid."

They have walked far enough. He is visibly upset, and Claire has had enough, but there is a question that has still gone unanswered. "Did you ever love Norah?"

"I wouldn't call it love."

She waits.

"I was obsessed with her," he continues. "She was different, smarter than I realized and she had no filter. Whatever she thought, she said." He chuckles, the lines of his face relax with memories. "Priests get accustomed to a certain amount of respect from their congregation, but I got none of that from Norah. She was interesting and thoughtful. I couldn't stop thinking about her. I wanted her, and clearly, she wanted me. But then you came, and our priorities changed, as they should have. She wanted a husband for her children, and I wanted the priesthood. At first, she wouldn't hear of adoption, but her brothers couldn't help her, and she had no choice. You were the one who came out ahead."

The wind stings her ears and nose. Seagulls with markings Claire has never seen before gather on the bluffs. She checks her watch. It is past time to go.

"Thank you for indulging me, and thank you for my transfusion. The choice was yours. You weren't obligated, and I'm grateful." She smiles. "God works in mysterious ways, doesn't He?"

"Yes, He does, Claire Williams. I'm very glad I got to meet you before I leave Tralee."

"Where are you going?"

"I haven't decided. There are quite a few places I haven't seen."

She holds out her hand. He takes it in both of his. "I wish you all the best, Father O'Sullivan."

"Thank you. I don't deserve your kindness, but I do appreciate it."

She nods and walks toward the car park without looking back.

THIRTY-SIX

Tralee, Co. Kerry, Ireland
~*Claire*

Claire buckles her seat belt and accepts the orange juice and warm bowl of mixed nuts from the flight attendant. The pain pill is taking effect, and she feels giddy at the idea of sleeping in her own bed in a little more than twelve hours.

Martin reaches over and rests his hand on her thigh. "How are you feeling?"

She smiles. "I'm delighted. Thank you for arranging everything, and thank you even more for coming to my rescue."

He lifts her hand and kisses it. "I'm atoning for my selfish behavior before you left. I'm so sorry, Claire. I've been spoiled, but it won't happen again."

"It's forgotten. I just want to go home, curl up in bed and sleep. Then I want to see Dad and the café, in that order."

"Don't be too hard on Michael."

"Are you kidding? I'm so grateful I'll probably kiss his feet."

~

Air traffic is light at John Wayne Airport, and for the first time in her life, there is no waiting to land the plane, nor is there a delay at the gate. Martin arranges for a wheelchair, and twenty minutes later they are in the car traveling down the 405 freeway toward home.

Claire turns off the air and presses the window control. The sun is warm on her arms and cheeks. She closes her eyes, grateful for heat, blue sky, five-lane freeways and mountains lining the horizon. Soon, very soon, she will be home.

~

She feels the mattress shift, but her eyelids are too heavy to open. "I'm not finished sleeping."

"You've been asleep for more than twenty-four hours, Claire. Your dad is here. He's going to think you're avoiding him."

She opens one eye.

Martin's voice is calm and filled with reason. "Are you avoiding him?"

"I don't think so."

"Why not get up, take a shower and talk to him? Even if you don't want to tackle the whole adoption issue, you can at least let him know you don't blame him for anything."

She sits up. "Is that what he thinks, that I blame him?"

"I have no idea. He's downstairs. Do you want me to tell him you're still sleeping?"

Shaking her head, she stands and heads for the bathroom. "No. Tell him I'll be down in fifteen minutes."

Claire pours shampoo into the palm of her hand, vowing never to take water pressure for granted again. She rinses twice, rubs in conditioner, rinses again and reluctantly reaches for the towel. Ten minutes later, dressed in linen slacks, a silk tunic and sandals, her wet hair pulled back with a clip, she walks downstairs toward voices on the patio. Her husband and her father are seated across from each other, a pitcher of iced tea on the table.

"Hi, Dad," she calls out.

He turns quickly, stands and meets her halfway. Searching her face, he holds out his arms. She walks into them. "Claire, you look wonderful. I was so worried. You've been through the wars, haven't you, sweetheart?"

She nods and blinks back tears. Martin stands and walks into the house, leaving them alone.

Michael O'Brian leads his daughter to the patio chair and sits down beside her. "Tell me what happened? Start wherever you like. Was it terrible?"

Claire shakes her head. "No, not really, at least not when Martin came. It just wasn't what I expected. Norah wasn't what I expected."

"What do you mean?"

Claire frowns. "I think you and Mom might have spoiled me, Dad."

"I'm losing focus here. How did we get from she wasn't what you expected to we spoiled you?"

"I thought she would be like Mom." Claire laughs shakily. "Norah isn't anything like her at all. She's remote, almost cold. Here I am, a child she gave birth to needing answers, and she simply refused to give me any. Her excuse for not telling me about my father was it would hurt *people*. More specifically, it would hurt him. Why should she care about someone who abandoned her when she was vulnerable? What about me? Does she think I haven't been hurt?" Her words spill out, raw and angry. "I have a sister, a real sister. You probably know that given what Norah told me about the night she gave me up. Her name is Brigid, and she isn't all that happy with Norah either. Her life hasn't been a piece of cake." Claire reaches for a tissue and blows her nose.

"All I originally wanted was to know why I was given up. I don't think that was an unreasonable request. She finally told me her reasons. I know about her hard life and how she had no money and no education, and no birth control. She said she was desperate and had no choice but to give me up. It was the Magdalene Laundries or complete community shame and ostracism."

Michael is silent.

Claire blows her nose again. "I wasn't mean to her if that's what you're thinking. I thanked her and went back to the hotel to call Martin. He figured out a way to find out who my birth father was. Then the car and I collided, and I was out of it until after the surgery. I just wanted to come home. Meanwhile, I learned that Norah and Brigid were tested to see if our blood types matched." She frowns. "It's so strange, Dad. Norah was willing to be my blood donor, but she wouldn't tell me who my birth father was. Then, because she couldn't be a donor, she took Martin to the church rectory to tell my birth father that he needed to be tested because I had to have blood for my surgery. She just did it, no questions asked, and he agreed, immediately, without coercion. I mean, who are these people? They don't want anything to do with me, and then they risk everything, all their secrets exposed, their anonymity, public opinion, their standing in the community to save my life."

Michael waits for her to finish.

"I don't know where I'm going with this."

"And I'm still not clear about the being spoiled part."

"I don't know why I'm angry. I have a great life. I always had a great life, thanks to you and Mom.

I lacked for nothing. Angry isn't the right word for how I feel. I'm bitter and, in a way, ashamed. Before I left, I saw him, Father O'Sullivan. We walked on the beach, and he told me he chose the priesthood over Norah. He was quite clear that he never loved her. He confessed his sins, apparently Norah and I were the sins, and his penance was to make sure we were taken care of and to bow completely out of our lives. He found you and Mom for me, and he found Norah a husband. He feels as if he's done his part."

She shakes her head. "You know, Dad, I think what upsets me is that I relate more to Patrick O'Sullivan and his jaded viewpoint than I do to Norah, despite her story of desperation. I see myself in him, not her, and she's the better person. That's where the spoiled comes in. Norah clearly didn't want to give me up." She looks at Michael. "I think you knew that, too. The question is, why didn't you ever tell me?"

"Ah," Michael O'Brian looks steadily at his daughter, the child of his heart but not his blood. "We come to the crux of the matter. It's not Norah or Patrick that you're angry with, and, yes, angry is the right word. You're angry with me." He shakes his head. "I never considered how important it would be for you to know where you came from. I thought if we loved you enough, you wouldn't need to find the parents whose gene pool you share. I thought you would settle in like Denis did. I was wrong. I owe you an explanation. But first, I have to answer your *'who are these people'* question. Norah O'Connor loved you desperately. Never doubt that. She tried every avenue available: her parents, her brothers, Child Protective Services, welfare, everything she could think of. Remember, she was on her own, ashamed of what she'd done, unable to tell anyone or ask for help. Her only experience with aid for pregnant mothers was Ireland's Magdalene Laundries, and she wouldn't consider that. When Father O'Sullivan stepped in to say he would find an adoptive family and she could more or less decide who adopted you, she agreed. Again, remember that your parents—all four of us— were products of their time and place in the world."

He holds out his hand, and she places hers in it. "While you waited in the taxi with Mom, I had a brief conversation with Norah. I gave her my card and told her to contact us if she needed anything." He shakes his head. "I had no idea that she would take me up on it."

Claire tenses. "What do you mean?"

"Two years later, just before your third birthday, Norah sent a letter addressed to your mother and me telling us she'd married and had the baby she was carrying. Her life had changed for the better, and she wanted you back. Mary opened it before I got home. She was horrified and justifiably furious with me for breaking one of the first rules of adoption; birth mothers shouldn't know the names and addresses of those who adopt their children. Mary wanted to find a lawyer immediately. I convinced her we weren't giving you up, but I wanted to try a different approach before we contacted lawyers."

"What was your different approach?"

"I made copies of home movies from the time we brought you home to the day we celebrated your third birthday and sent them all to Norah. I made sure she saw how you'd settled into your life with us, how you called for Mommy and then Daddy to push you in your new swing, how you laughed hysterically when Denis ran around the yard with you in the wheelbarrow. I filmed your grandparents holding you on your first Halloween when Mom made your princess costume. I filmed our Thanksgiving dinners and Christmas mornings." He stopped. "Are you crying?"

Claire laughs. "Yes, and so are you. What happened then?"

Her father shrugs and smiles. "I don't know. I never heard from her again. What I do know is that by no stretch of the imagination is Norah Malone a remote or cold woman. Her love is limitless. She wouldn't uproot you again, no matter how much she wanted to have you with her. I've no doubt that it caused her great pain to leave you with us, but she saw that we were a family. I'll be forever grateful."

Claire's tears spill down her cheeks. "Those were great times, Dad, and so were all the times after."

Michael gathers her close. "They were fabulous times."

"I'm so glad you didn't give me back."

"That was never going to happen."

A minute passes, then two. Claire pulls her father's handkerchief, always within reach, out of his breast pocket and blows her nose. "So, Dad. Shall I fix the three of us some food?"

He laughs. "That's my girl. I thought you'd never ask."

THIRTY-SEVEN

San Juan Capistrano, California
Six months later

"Hi, Aunt Claire." Liz walks through the door of
the café, shrugs out of her jacket and hangs it on the
back of a chair. "I hope I'm not interrupting, but I
wanted to see you in person." She looks around at the
cornflower blue and yellow walls, the new prints and
the rich burnished copper of the pots gleaming from
the cook's station to the patio. "The place looks great.
I've been away too long."

Claire smiles. "It's always a pleasure to visit with
my favorite niece. What's up?"

"I won. I got the apprenticeship."

"That's great, Liz." Her face registers no more than
polite interest.

"Are you even aware of what I'm talking about?"

Claire taps her chin with a pencil. "Vaguely."

Liz frowns. "Don't you remember that I asked if I could shoot a video of your blog for my class project?"

"Hmmm. Which project?"

Liz's face falls. "Are you serious? This is the most important thing that's ever happened to me, and you don't even remember. You *should* remember. I got this because of you."

She chuckles. "Relax, Lizzie. Have a cup of my delicious, locally roasted coffee. Of course, I'm not serious. I'm teasing you. What happened to your sense of humor?"

"That's a relief." Liz sits, her disappointment forgotten and leans across the small table Claire favors. Her eyes sparkle. "I have great news."

Claire waits in anticipation. Finally, she asks. "Are you going to tell me?"

"Guess."

"Come on. Just tell me. I'm dying to know."

Liz breathes deeply. "*My project won*. What I'm trying to say is, *your blog won*. Because of your blog, I have a summer internship at The School of Culinary Arts in Dublin. I got a full ride."

Claire stares at her. "TU? In Dublin? When did this happen? I thought it was a class project. You said nothing about an apprenticeship."

"My professor sent my video to Dublin. They got back to me this week. I didn't want to tell you in case it didn't happen."

"Does your dad know?"

"Of course, he knows. I told Mom first, and then I told him. You were next on the list."

"I'm flattered, really, I am, but is he okay with it? He wasn't thrilled when you first mentioned giving up college for a culinary apprenticeship."

"I'm not giving up college. Like you said, most people already have a degree when they apply. This is an apprenticeship, a summer program. Be happy for me, Aunt Claire."

Claire stands and holds out her arms. "I'm so happy that I'm going to give you a congratulatory hug, and then we'll celebrate. Come here, my brilliant, beautiful niece." She hugs her fiercely. "I am thrilled for you. You are amazing and a chip off the old block if I do say so myself."

Liz steps back. "You're really pleased, right?"

"I'm ecstatic."

Liz breathes what can only be a sigh of relief. "Dad said I had to get your approval."

Claire frowns. "That's odd. Did he tell you why?"

"Not in so many words. I think it has to do with your trip to Ireland."

"Liz, are you sure you're telling me everything?"

"I really think you should ask Dad. I'm not at all in the loop."

"In that case, that's what I'll do. Meanwhile, we'll celebrate with your masterpiece, a signature chocolate soufflé served with orange crème anglaise."

Claire climbs the wide marble steps leading to the pristine glass and steel structure where her brother spends his days practicing corporate law. She looks around at the intimidating surroundings and suppresses a slight shudder. Fashion Island is beautiful but cold. It's been a while since she's met Denis for lunch.

The new receptionist smiles at her. "You must be Claire."

"That's right. How did you know?"

"You and Mr. O'Brian look very much alike."

Claire's eyes widen. Clearly, Denis does not share personal information with his employees. "Actually, not that much," she replies. "It's nice to meet you."

"I could see it in a minute." She gestures at the forbidding floor-to-ceiling doors. "Mr. O'Brian is in the conference room. Please, go right in. He's alone."

Claire opens the door and closes it behind her. The room is spacious, and the conference table is the largest she's ever seen. The chairs, she counts thirty of them, are ergonomic and plush. "This is the most terrifying room I've ever seen."

Denis lifts his head and laughs. "I know it's not your thing, but it ceases to be intimidating after a few weeks. Was there traffic?"

"Not too bad. I took the coast road. The beach is beautiful. I love seeing it off-season."

"Then you'll appreciate where we're eating. I made reservations at The Rooftop. It's a perfect day. Do you mind?"

"Of course not."

"Thanks for coming to me, Claire. I've got a lot on my plate right now."

"Liz told me about the apprenticeship. I wanted to ask you about it."

"Ask away but let's talk and eat at the same time. I don't want to rush through our food."

~

The Rooftop is busy as usual with comfortable seating, lush plants and a diamond-bright view of the Pacific that people pay fortunes to call home. Their table is secluded, the wine on ice and the service excellent and discreet. Claire slips on her sunglasses, sips her wine and smiles at her brother. "This is perfect, Denis. Now, tell me, how are you?"

"Today, I'm showing off. You don't come around very often."

"I guess not. It's probably because I never want this to get old."

"It never does." He clears his throat. "Liz told me she broke the news to you."

"Yes, she did. I'm very happy for her. In fact, I'm taking credit for her love of cooking."

"But?—"

"I'm wondering why you changed your mind. You were adamantly opposed to cooking school for Liz the last time she brought it up. What happened?"

Denis picks up his wine glass and sits back. "I had no problem with her goal of becoming a chef. I was opposed to her dropping out of college. This is a summer apprenticeship. She'll come home and, hopefully, finish school. Meanwhile, she's got the summer to figure out if she has a real affinity for chopping, as you once called it."

"So why the condition that I approve?"

"Because Liz will be going to Ireland. We haven't yet talked about your time in Ireland."

"I don't understand."

"You left home determined to meet your birth mother. Then you came back and said nothing about her at all. What happened in Ireland, Claire?"

She stares out over the ocean. Swells of blue ocean glitter under the afternoon sun while tiny sandpipers dash madly across the wet sand in their quest for hermit crabs and periwinkles. She waits for the ache in her chest, followed by tears that rise up and spill over whenever she thinks of Norah. But they don't, not even when she calls up the memory of a young Norah O'Connor leaving Boston, her child in the arms of Mary O'Brian, the mother who could always be talked into an ice cream cone or one more bedtime story, the woman who walked her to school and designed Halloween costumes, who made every birthday an event and bought season tickets for the children she taught to love show tunes.

"Claire? Are you with me?"

"Denis, sorry. I was thinking of Mom. Remember when you told me you weren't interested in finding your birth mother because you already had a great mother?"

He nods.

"She was my mother, too, and you were right. She was a great mother. It took finding Norah Malone to make me realize that not only did I not miss anything at all, I actually lucked out. I have no regrets, but I am going to work at seeing Dad as often as I can. He's pretty special, too. In fact, we had and still have a terrific family, including my talented niece. Martin and I are talking about a trip to Dublin while she's there. How about coming with us?"

Denis laughs. "Have you been talking to my wife? She's been working on me ever since Liz spilled the beans."

"I haven't, but great minds …"

"All right, all right. You know my idea of a vacation is the Bahamas or Tahiti. But I suppose I could bend a little this year."

"You could also reap a bit of culture."

"Now, you sound like Mom."

"That's the nicest compliment you could ever give me."

THANK YOU FOR READING MY BOOK!

Dear Reader,

I hope you enjoyed *Birthright*.

As an author, I value getting feedback. I would love to hear what your favorite part was, and what you liked or disliked, please share your thoughts with me. You can write me at jeanetteb53@gmail.com.

Also, I'd like to ask a favor. If you are so inclined, please write a review of *Birthright* on Amazon and Goodreads. You, the reader, have the power to influence other readers to share your journey with a book you've read. In fact, most readers pick their next book because of a review or on the advice of a friend. So, please share! You can find all of my books on my Amazon author page.

Thank you so much for reading *Birthright*, and thanks for spending time with me and my story.

Best regards,

Jeanette Baker

www.jeanettebaker.com
facebook.com/jeanette.baker.77

About the Author

Jeanette Baker is the award-winning author of twenty paranormal, historical and contemporary novels, most of them set in the lush countryside of Southwest Ireland where she lives with her husband and writes during the "Seasons of Silence," the autumn and winter months. Her ancestors, the O'Flahertys, hail from the counties of Kerry and Galway. She takes great pride in the prayer posted by the English over the ancient city gates, "From the wrath of the O'Flahertys, may the good Lord deliver us."

Jeanette spent many years teaching sixth grade in a small school nestled under a canopy of eucalyptus trees where the children consistently surprised her with their wisdom, their hopefulness and their enthusiasm for great stories. Currently, she enjoys the company of her own grown children and her precious grandchildren.

Jeanette graduated from the University of California at Irvine and holds a Master's Degree in Education.

She is the Rita award-winning author of *NELL*.